PIGASUS

THE LOST PARADISE ELYSIUM
BATTLE FOR EVERMORE

WITH THE FAITH TO BELIEVE IN LOVE

PIGASUS
THE LOST PARADISE ELYSIUM
BATTLE FOR EVERMORE

Written and Created by
Donald James McDowell

Creative Illustrations by
Brendon Saumure &
Donald James McDowell

Artwork by
Brendon Saumure &
Ashley Thompson

Layout and Design by
Brady Keeler

McD's Mountain
Music Publishing

MCD'S MOUNTAIN PUBLISHING PRESENTS PIGASUS First Printing. Copyright McD's Mountain Publishing LLC 2020.
ALL RIGHTS RESERVED. Published by McD's Mountain Publishing

ISBN: 978-1-77135-287-1   Printed in China

In the beginning, long, long ago, in a time before time there was a most wondrous land. A paradise known as the land of Elysium, which co-existed with the lands of all that was. The peaceful tranquility of Elysium flourished. It was a time of love and beauty known since the beginning. Nowhere was Elysium as beautiful as in Shasta valley below the towering twin peaks of the ancient volcano Shasta.

It was here, on the night of the full blue moon of Elysium, where the all-powerful-all knowing Presence came to visit all He loves. In the pass between the peaks, a wondrous waterfall flowed from a towering cliff across a large cave, which was the gateway to Elysium.

The brilliant blue light of Elysium was glowing from the other side of the portal, creating a misty rainbow across the falls. It was here that the mighty Rintrah, a magnificent Lion with wings and piercing blue eyes, had his lair in the cave behind the falls, where he stood steadfast on the cliff above with his watchful eyes, as Rintrah has always been the guardian of the gateway to Elysium.

On this rarest of nights, the loving light of the Presence comes to welcome those entering the paradise Elysium. All who believe, take the Leap of Faith, accepting His loving light into their hearts, knowing that "With the Faith to Believe in Love, Life becomes Magic".

This was also when the Presence would visit His most cherished creations; the mighty Pegasus and the beautiful Unicorn, guardians of the paradise Elysium. The mystical Pegasus was entrusted with the powers of light and defender of truth, honor and justice.

The magical Unicorn was gifted the powers of love and defender of faith, hope, love and family. As the brilliant colored lights of Elysium began to swirl through the midnight sky above the valley Shasta and the full blue moon was centered high above the towering twin peaks of Elysium. The mighty Rintrah roars from the cliff edge above the cave beneath the East peak of Shasta. All was as it should be.

Since the beginning, Once every thousand years, the Presence would visit Shasta Valley and appear within the large ancient oak, which stood alone on a small hill in the pasture below the towering twin peaks of Mt. Shasta. Only on this night, the night of the full blue moon, when the fires burned blue and the wondrous lights of Elysium swirled across the midnight sky could Unicorn and Pegasus be together within the light of the Presence.

In this lush meadow, which was their home, would they again declare their endless love for one another, and each renew their commitment to always loving the Presence. Unicorn and Pegasus would once again take their Leap of Faith into His loving light. It was a special time, a time of renewal, a time of commitment to all that is true – to all that is good – to all that is Faith, Hope, Love & Family.

On the night of the seventh millennium the Presence was so touched by the love found in the eyes of the mystical Pegasus and the magical Unicorn that he blessed them with a daughter, to be known as Unisus. With rainbow colored wings like her father and magical golden horn, main, tail and fetlocks like her mother, the beautiful Unisus was truly blessed by the Presence. She too would follow Unicorn & Pegasus with her first Leap of Faith into the loving light of the Presence.

On the night of the ninth millennium the Presence warned of the tenth millennium. It was foretold that there would come into the paradise Elysium an evil one, known only as Rathvar, who would come from the blackness of the darkness to challenge all that is true, all that is good and all that they loved. There would be a great battle, a battle for evermore between good and evil.

When the tenth millennium came, it again brought the return of the full blue moon and the Presence, who once again came to Shasta valley to be with those He loved. His loving light illuminating the ancient oak beneath the majestic twin peaks of Mt. Shasta. Once again glorified by the faith, hope and love found in the hearts of Unicorn, Pegasus and Unisus, the Presence welcomed their Leap of Faith followed by the mighty roar of Rintrah.

But, after their leap of faith into His loving light, a strange darkness began to fall over the land. As the lights of Elysium faded, the winds began to blow, the night turned cold and the moon became as the blackness of the darkness. The evil Rathvar had come and a great battle ensued.

It began with the total eclipse of the full blue moon. A great storm grew atop the twin peaks darkening the light and spreading the blackness of the darkness across the land. Rathvar soon appeared on the highest west peak of the ancient volcano Shasta. He came as the darkest of shadows on the blackest of nights. Black lightning arched across the sky and thunder rumbled through the valley. Just as it seemed that the blackness of the darkness that was spreading throughout the land would engulf all that was, a brilliant blue light appeared high above the twin peaks of Elysium.

A new storm began to grow from that light. The skies began to rumble, and blue lightning flashed throughout the depths of the storm. Below, on the west peak, black lightning flashed within the evil storm of Rathvar's rage.

Suddenly all became quiet. All became still. Then from the boundless depths of the light within the new storm, a loud rumbling began to grow throughout the sky. It grew and grew. The ground began to shake. As the mighty storm became the brilliant light of the Presence, a magnificent bolt of blue lightning came from deep within the storm and struck the evil Rathvar. The ancient volcano erupted in a violent storm, leaving only the depths of a great crater, once the towering west peak of Mt. Shasta.

The blackness of his darkness was gone, but so too was paradise lost and the loving light of the Presence vanished. As the sun began to rise from behind Mt Shasta it became all too clear what had been foretold had now come to pass. The evil Rathvar was gone. Unicorn, Pegasus and Unisus were gone. The twin peaks of Elysium were no more.

Now only the East peak remained, and a great crater replaced the once towering west peak of Mt. Shasta, now and forever a reminder of the evil Rathvar, the great battle and paradise lost. The wondrous waterfall and the light of Elysium were gone and the barren limbs of the sacred oak in the valley below made it all too clear that the beautiful paradise Elysium was gone. All that was, was no more.

The great storm passed and as the last lights of Elysium faded into the light of day. The Presence foretold of a time ten millenniums from this day of another great battle, the battle for evermore, when the evil Rathvar would again appear to spread the blackness of his darkness throughout the land.

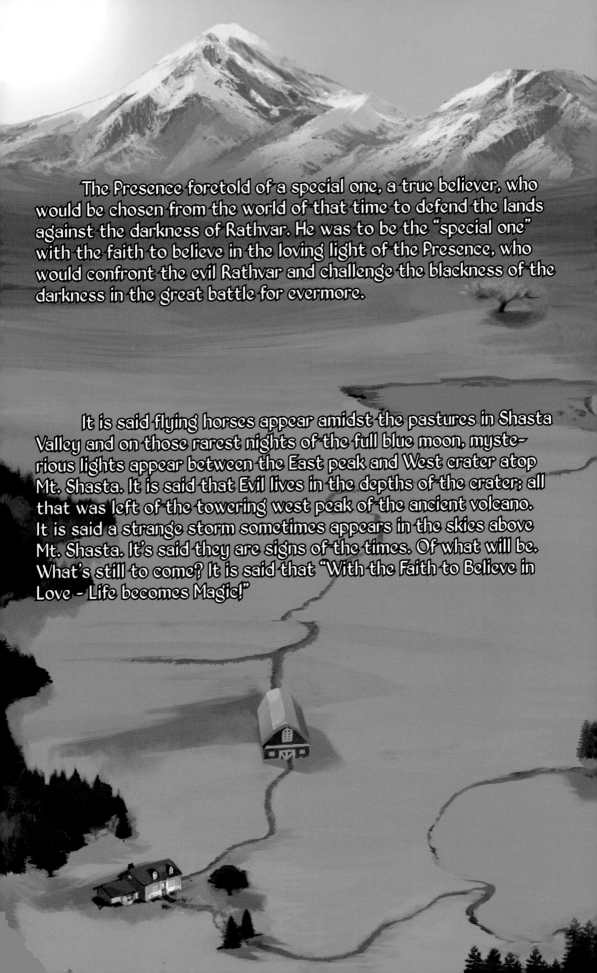

The Presence foretold of a special one, a true believer, who would be chosen from the world of that time to defend the lands against the darkness of Rathvar. He was to be the "special one" with the faith to believe in the loving light of the Presence, who would confront the evil Rathvar and challenge the blackness of the darkness in the great battle for evermore.

It is said flying horses appear amidst the pastures in Shasta Valley and on those rarest nights of the full blue moon, mysterious lights appear between the East peak and West crater atop Mt. Shasta. It is said that Evil lives in the depths of the crater; all that was left of the towering west peak of the ancient volcano. It is said a strange storm sometimes appears in the skies above Mt. Shasta. It's said they are signs of the times. Of what will be. What's still to come? It is said that "With the Faith to Believe in Love - Life becomes Magic!"

Ten millenniums passed. It's now springtime in Shasta Valley and the majestic Mt. Shasta towers high in the sky above what was once Elysium. There's a small ranch near the base of the ancient volcano, where the Bennett family lives George, Ruth, their children Johnny, Becky and Mawdy, Becky' rag doll.

Their house with its whitewashed fence stands beside a big red barn and across the creek is the old shack where the aged caretaker Amostis lives. A little further is an unusually large old oak tree, which stands alone atop a small hill overlooking the lush pasture, where Clem Clopper, Ruth's very old buckskin, enjoys its shade. Snuggle Bunny, the families pet bunny rabbit was scampering through Ruth's garden. It was a typical, beautiful spring day in Shasta valley.

But springs new life also brought fate, as Becky finds a little runt piglet abandoned near the barn. "Oh, my! Look Mawdy!" Becky said to her rag doll. "That poor little piggy needs our help!" She thought he was so cute and lovingly picked him up and carries him into the house to have her mother help and show her how to take care of the little runt pig.

As Becky entered the front door, she quickly made her way to the kitchen. "Look Mommy! Mawdy and I found this cute little piggy by the fence. Can we keep him Mommy? Please! He needs us."

As Becky holds the fragile piglet up, she notices his nose. "Look Mawdy, he has a heart shaped nose! It's so cute!" The little piglet looked up at Becky and seemed to smile at her amazement.

"Oh, My Becky! He's so small." Ruth carefully took the little pig from Becky's hands and placed him in a basket with a warm blanket next to the fire. As the little runt pig seemed to snuggle into the blanket, he struggled to look up at Ruth, Becky & Mawdy.

Becky smiled lovingly, "Mommy look! He's giving Snuggle Bunny 'Tuggles'!" Tuggles were like cuddling bunny hugs, as he nuzzled his nose against you. "Mommy, we have to keep him now. We just have too!"

"Rebecca Lynn, we just can't keep a runt pig, there is no time for such nonsense. After supper we will take him out and you can leave him with old Clem." George said sternly.

Ruth looked at Becky, who was now "tuggling" Mawdy and then looked over at George with a small tear beginning to well up in her eyes. "Oh, George!"

But Becky is not allowed to keep the "little Piggy", which was near death. Her father won't let her. George knew this was only going to get harder. In his heart, he felt he was doing the right thing, as he knew the little runt pig wouldn't survive the night. "It's time." George declared and with that he started towards the basket.

But Becky & Mawdy grabbed it first and as she did, pulled it close to her heart and both Snuggle Bunny and the little pig were nuzzling up against Mawdy and Becky. "Mawdy and me, we sure love you, yes we do!" Becky whispered softly.

That evening, Unisus, knowing it was the special night foretold, returned to Shasta Valley to see "The Special One". She secretly watched Becky lead the entire family, including Snuggle Bunny, out towards the pasture to "let nature take its course".

As they crossed the small bridge across the creek, Amostis, who was the old caretaker that lived in the small cabin next to the bridge, was standing in the middle of it looking up at the ancient volcano. "Amostis, look at our little piggy, isn't he cute!" Becky said still innocently naive of what was happening! She lifted the basket up to show him.

Amostis gazed down to see the little piglet and realized how near death he was. "Oh, my, my" he said sadly, then as the piglet looks up at him and tries to smile, clearly very weak. "Why your little piggy has a heart shaped nose, Becky, yep he surely does."

Becky smiled and innocently says "We are taking him out to the pasture. Daddy says we have to let nature take its course"

"Don't you worry none Becky old Clem Clopper will watch over him." With that, Amostis headed on back to his cabin and the Bennett family continued across the bridge into the lush spring grass where they saw old Clem over by the oak tree that stood alone in the pasture beside the creek. Becky insisted that they leave the pig with Clem so that he would not be alone.

"Clem Clopper" Becky said sternly, "This little Piggy is very special, and you simply must stay close and watch over him." Then, Becky set down the basket under the protective branches of the oak in the tall grass at Clem's feet. Becky then started to cry, as the runt pig laid there looking up at her, struggling to breath.

This brought tears to Ruth's eyes and there was even a hint of tears in Mawdy's Blue-Button eyes. Even though George stood firm with his decision, he is visibly moved by his daughter's tears, while Johnny stands fast trying not to get choked up, but clearly, he is. Even Snuggle Bunny has little bunny tears in his eyes.

There in front of Snuggle Bunny lay the small, dying little runt piglet looking helplessly up at them. "Becky, it's time to say goodbye." George proclaimed.

Becky rushed over to her little piggy and carefully picks him up out of the blanket filled basket and says "Oh, Little Piggy, We Love You". Becky then ran her fingers gently across his face and Mawdy gave him a heartfelt tuggle. There is a brief glimmer of hope & love in the eyes of little pig, as Becky leans forward to nuzzle her nose against his nose. Then she gently laid the runt piglet in the tall grass beneath the old oak tree.

"Oh, Daddy" Becky cried, and she quickly leans down and snuggles the piglet with one last tuggle, when we hear her little piggy whisper in her ear in "Baby Tongue" to barely utter "Becky, I Love You Too". We see Becky's eyes begin to glimmer in surprise.

But just as she realizes the little runt piglet is talking to her, George grabs Becky by the arm and pulls her back next to hm. "I'm sorry Becky, but we talked about this. We can't keep a little runt pig and we have to let nature take its course" The little pig seemed to try and hold on to her, but he is much too weak and though he wants to reach out to her he can't and slumps back into the tall grass.

Ruth reaches over and takes Becky's other hand and looks down to her with the loving eyes that only a mother can share with her daughter in tender moments like this, "Becky – Sweetie – We've done all we can for him – he is in God's hands now. He knows you Love him very much and we will make sure and say a "Special Prayer" for him, OK Baby".

This seemed to comfort Becky & Mawdy a little, as she leaned over and pressed her cheek against her mother's leg. With that they all turned sadly away from the dying little runt pig and as Becky looked over her shoulder with her tear covered cheeks, we see him struggling for what are surely his last breaths as a tear forms in his eyes. It's more than Becky & Mawdy can bear and they again burst into tears.

As they all walk back towards the house, we see Clem Clopper just as a big old tear falls to the ground, knowing the end is near for the little runt pig. Clem turns and slowly takes a few steps towards Shasta and looks high into the sky above its East peak, as if to be asking or looking for some kind of divine intervention. Then Clem lowers his head as a big old Clopper tear fell into the tall grass.

Later that night, the curious Unisus went to Becky's window, secretly watching as Becky and Mawdy pray for God to save her little Piggy's life. Becky folds her hands and closes her eyes to say a very special prayer, "Dear God, Bless Mommy and Daddy and Mawdy and umm, my brother Johnny and Please, Oh Please God, Bless my little Piggy".

As Becky is praying, we begin to see the intense blue light and swirling gold dust of the Presence appear in the ceiling corner behind her. As Becky continues to pray, we see it becoming brighter & brighter. "He's so small and we Love him so much. Mommy always says, "With the Faith to Believe in Love ~ Life becomes Magic".

Becky hesitated and opened her eyes to see Mawdy's Blue Button eyes strangely sparkling. Becky just smiled, closed her eyes again and continued, "Dear God, Mawdy and me, We Believe and We Love You! Amen!

As Ruth turns out the lantern light, we see Unisus, looking in with a tear of love in her eyes. Then suddenly there was a flash of brilliant blue lightning that seemed to light up the night sky and as the thunder echoed through the valley, she turns her eyes back towards the pasture.

Then another mighty bolt of blue lightning arched through a growing storm above Shasta with the thundering sound shaking the ground beneath her feet. Unisus bolts towards the ancient oak, galloping as fast as she could, leaving a trail of magical golden dust behind her.

As she thunders towards the small hill in the pasture, another brilliant bolt of blue lightning lights the night sky and the thunder rolls through Shasta valley. Old Clem Clopper raises his head and turns to see Unisus, just as she abruptly comes to a halt. She was standing right where the Bennett family had stood earlier in front of the ancient oak. Not even acknowledging that Clem was nearby, her entire focus was on the struggling little piggy laying in the tall grass just in front of her.

Unisus lowered her head for a closer look, and saw the poor little runt piglet gasping for every breath. "Oh, No!" she said, as she realized how desperate the situation was. "I am too late". Unisus slowly lowers her head and gently nuzzles the little piglet with her warm wet nose. As a tear falls into the tall grass, she is certain these are the dying little piglets last breaths.

All of a Sudden! "Whee-Heeeeee-Heeeee-Heeeeee!"

Startled, Unisus leapt back from the dying pig. Clem froze in his tracks. "Wheeeee-Heeee-Heeeee", they heard it again. Clem whirled around, looked up into the sky where he had heard the noise and to his astonishment, he saw the mighty Pegasus and the beautiful Unicorn above the age old Oak tree.

It was an incredible sight to see them flying through the night sky by the light of the rising full moon. Behind the magical golden dust trailing from the fetlocks of Unicorn you could see the towering ancient volcano Shasta.

As foretold so long ago, the full blue moon of Elysium rose high above Shasta's peak beside the Big Dipper and Becky's prayers are answered, when just as the little piggy was on his final breath, Unicorn & Pegasus land beside him as the light of the Presence appears in the ancient oak tree.

Clem Clopper was awestruck as they landed next to the dying little runt pig only a short distance away. First Pegasus with his magnificent strong wings and then Unicorn with her beautiful golden mane and tail brilliantly glistening in the moonlight.

Old Clem began to slowly back up, intrigued yet bewildered. Pegasus looked old Clem right in the eye and seemed to re-assure him that everything would be all right.

Off in the distance, we hear thunder and Clem looks up to see a single storm cloud above the south end of the valley and seemed to be heading straight for Mt. Shasta. Unicorn took several steps toward the pig until she stood next to him. She looked up towards Shasta and saw the "Lights of Elysium" begin to brighten above the East peak, as the full moon rises above Shasta. Unicorn then looked at her daughter and said, "Unisus, he is the Special One".

Then the magical Unicorn looked down at the runt piglet, raised her golden tail above him and sprinkled the magical Golden dust of Elysium over the helpless little piggy. It fell over him and then started to swirl about him. Unicorn then stepped back, and mighty Pegasus stepped towards the runt pig.

He too turned to face the mountain and looked up to see the now spectacular sight of the full moon above Shasta and the brilliant "Lights of Elysium". Strangely the storm had near centered over the top of Shasta, the only cloud in the sky. A large bolt of blue lightning crackled through the clouds from within making the entire storm appear blue.

Pegasus turned back towards the little pig, spread his mighty rainbow colored wings and then slowly arched them forward. When the wing tips of Pegasus touched one another, an intense bolt of brilliantly blue lightning appeared from the wings of Pegasus and struck the little runt pig. As it did, a deafening thunder could be heard atop the mountain.

Pegasus and Unicorn both turned to face the mountain and as they did a brilliant blue light began to glow around the pig and it grew and grew until he was completely engulfed in the intense blue light with gold dust swirling throughout.

The little runt pig began to rise above the grass and miraculously floated up and atop the mystical Pegasus and sat suspended in midair between his mighty rainbow colored wings.

Once there, Unicorn and Pegasus turned to face one another centered in front of the tree with Shasta in the background. The dying little runt piglet had been saved, miraculously touched by the light of the Presence.

They both looked over at Unisus and old Clem. The astounded Clem could only grin, but it was from ear to ear, as he knew what he had seen was a miracle. They then turned to face the mountain and after a brief pause of silence, the mighty Pegasus bolted into the night sky and the beautiful Unicorn reared back and leaped into the air behind her beloved Pegasus.

As quickly as they had appeared, Unisus and old Clem Clopper watched Unicorn, Pegasus and the little runt pig soaring high into the night sky. As they flew towards the ancient volcano Shasta, Clem could see them silhouetted in the center of the full moon, as they seemed to be flying towards it.

They could see the magical Unicorn with the faint golden dust trailing behind her as she galloped through the night sky. At her side, the mystical Pegasus with the runt pig still nestled in the blue light glowing between his magnificent rainbow colored wings.

In the pass beneath the East peak, the brilliant blue light of the Presence is filling the opening of the big old cave that everyone knew about. But tonight, it wasn't just an old cave. It was alive with the loving light of the Presence and a beautiful waterfall flowing from the cliff above.

It is in fact a mystical gateway! A magical portal to enter into the lost paradise Elysium and standing majestically on the cliff above, is the mighty Rintrah. "Rrrooaarrr!" Unicorn & Pegasus saved the dying runt piglet, flying him through the mystical portal, guarded by the mighty Rintrah and into their magical paradise Elysium.

Back in the pasture, Unisus is confused as she walks to the spot beneath the ancient oak talking to herself. "It can't be? A pig is the special one? He can't save us from the evil Rathvar." As Unisus bolts into the night sky, she says "He can't even fly?" She couldn't accept fate had chosen a little runt pig to be the "Special One".

Old Clem couldn't believe his eyes. He could only watch in awe, as Unisus flew towards Mt. Shasta. As she vanished through the portal to Elysium, the mighty Rintrah's roar echoed thru the valley. "Rrrooaarrrr!" All was as it should be.

Now safe in Elysium, Unicorn, Pegasus and Unisus gracefully land at the base of the ancient oak tree, identical to the one on the Bennett ranch in Shasta valley with the twin peaks of Mt. Shasta towering high above. Pegasus slides the piglet safely down his wing gently into the lush green grass beneath the tree.

The baby pig settles into the tall green grass, slightly arching his back, stretching his little feet together, his legs touching at the peak of the stretch. His tiny mouth opens in a runt-sized yawn that makes his heart-shaped nose twitch a little. Opening his eyes, seeing grass for the first time, which he curiously sniffs and tickles his nose. With a smile, the little piggy tries to stand, one foot, a second, third, and forth, and "THUMP", he falls on his side.

He attempts to stand again, getting to all four legs shakily just long enough for a brief pause of triumph mixed with curiosity. But, once again, his front legs slide out from under him and "SPLAT", falls again, his rear and curly tail in the air.

The little runt pig stands again and as he does, discovers a strange curiosity on his rump. A curly thing that as he looked at it, it wiggled! That was exciting and he wanted a closer look. As he turned his head, he began to turn and the harder he tried to get a closer look at the curly curiosity, the more he turned until he was chasing his tail in circles. Around and around, which made him very dizzy and he again fell to the ground.

Looking around, his eyes rest on the ancient oak towering above. A blue light begins to glow from the heart of the tree, glowing larger and more intense, golden particles appearing and swirling within. It was the Loving Light of the Presence. The piglet was mesmerized.

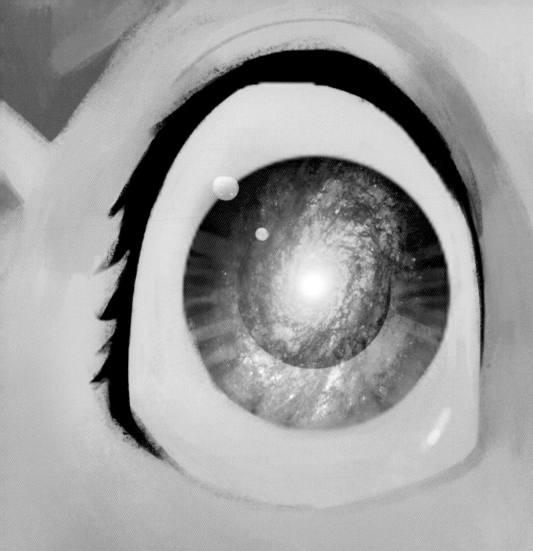

Reflected in his eyes is the brilliant blue light with golden particles swirling within, then the golden particles faded, and the brilliant blue light turns from a reflection into the actual "Blue" color of his eyes.

The piglet, now with beautiful blue eyes, continues staring in wonderment into the light of the Presence coming from the heart of the tree, unaware that Unicorn, Pegasus and Unisus are still standing behind him.

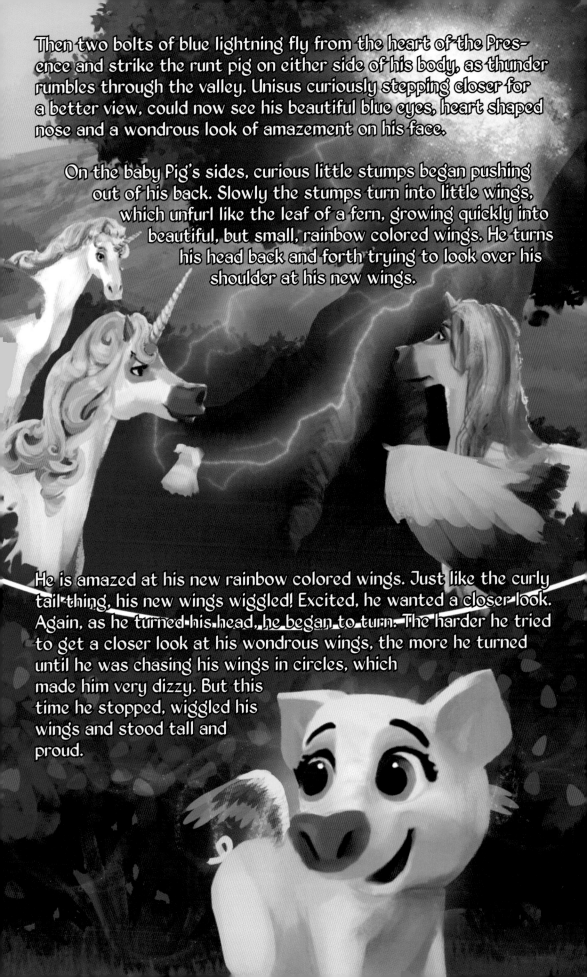

Then two bolts of blue lightning fly from the heart of the Presence and strike the runt pig on either side of his body, as thunder rumbles through the valley. Unisus curiously stepping closer for a better view, could now see his beautiful blue eyes, heart shaped nose and a wondrous look of amazement on his face.

On the baby Pig's sides, curious little stumps began pushing out of his back. Slowly the stumps turn into little wings, which unfurl like the leaf of a fern, growing quickly into beautiful, but small, rainbow colored wings. He turns his head back and forth trying to look over his shoulder at his new wings.

He is amazed at his new rainbow colored wings. Just like the curly tail thing, his new wings wiggled! Excited, he wanted a closer look. Again, as he turned his head, he began to turn. The harder he tried to get a closer look at his wondrous wings, the more he turned until he was chasing his wings in circles, which made him very dizzy. But this time he stopped, wiggled his wings and stood tall and proud.

Unicorn and Pegasus continued watching, surprised that now the little runt pig was looking a little chubby, they both smiled. Then the little pig, looking back at his left wing, giving it a tentative flap. FLAP. Then looking back at his right wing, giving it a tentative flap. FLAP!

Unisus began to laugh when the now plump little pig, with a look of concentration on his face, begins attempting to flap both his wings. But the wings aren't flapping together. They flap left then right, left then right (1-2, 1-2, 1-2, and so on). A shy, but naively proud smile comes across his face, as they beat faster and faster. But still out of sequence (1-2, 1-2, 1-2, etc....).

Amazingly Unisus watched as his feet slowly leave the ground, but only a tiny bit, only to clumsily land again. His front legs slide out from under him again and we see him again plop to the ground. His curly tail and rear in the air along with the now slowly beating wings, pulsing out of sequence. The little pig is clearly exhausted from his "flight".

It was then, after Unicorn, Pegasus & Unisus watched the baby pig receive his amazing gifts of blue eyes and rainbow colored wings, that Pegasus looked the piglet right in the eyes and proudly gave him his name saying, "PIGASUS! Your name shall be PIGASUS!

The tired piggy smiled in innocent satisfaction. Pigasus sighs and lets his rear legs slide onto the ground, too. Like a little puppy, he curls around himself, his wings resting against his body. With a content smile and a long sigh, the piglet snuggles into the tall grass of Elysium where he falls quickly asleep.

Unicorn and Pegasus looked down at that cute little pig, then looked deep into the Light of the Presence, before turning to face their daughter and the doubt in her eyes, that this littlepig could be the "Special One", chosen by fate to do battle against the evil Rathvar in the coming Battle for Evermore.

After a moment of silence, the mighty Pegasus spoke, "Unisus you must always remember, "With the Faith to Believe in Love – Life becomes Magic!"

Then Unicorn and Pegasus looked lovingly into each other's eyes, just before rearing back and leaping into the night. The mighty rainbow colored wings of Pegasus carried him high into the Elysium sky with a long trail of magical golden dust trailing behind the beautiful Unicorn as she galloped closely behind. Unisus watched, as they flew off towards the full blue moon above the towering twin peaks of Mt Shasta.

Unisus remained, now starring at the little pig with beautiful blue eyes and rainbow colored wings, all snuggled up sleeping in the tall grass of Elysium.

"Pigasus", she said quietly, still finding it hard to believe that this could be the "Special One".

"Pigasus! A pig with wings and he still can't even fly!" But Unisus was a true believer. Even though she wondered, "How is that cute little piggy ever going to defeat the evil Rathvar", she had faith.

"Pigasus", she whispered, so as not to wake him, "With the Faith to Believe in Love Life becomes Magic!"

Unisus then looked lovingly into the light of the Presence, reared back and bolted into the night sky. Her rainbow colored wings gracefully carried her towards Mt. Shasta and a magical trail of golden dust followed, as she galloped towards the full blue moon of Elysium.

The next morning back at the Bennett's ranch, Becky and Mawdy couldn't hardly wait to go out to the pasture to see their little Piggy. As they all finished breakfast, the family gathered on the front porch.

"You know kids, nature has its ways and him being the runt pig and all ----" George hesitated, as he saw the excited look in Becky's eyes, "Well, I just don't want you to get your hopes up too high."

Becky blurted out "But, Daddy, Mawdy and me, we said special prayers for the little piggy and asked God to keep him safe and–."

Ruth looked at Becky, then Mawdy and back into Becky's big blue eyes and said "You and Mawdy said our special prayer? About faith and love ––"

Becky interrupted "–– and believing. Didn't we Mawdy". "Well then Becky, I believe God will keep him safe. Let's all go get that little piggy." Ruth said smiling at their innocence.

They all began slowly walking towards the pasture. Looking towards the old oak tree, they could see the sun shining above Mt. Shasta and old Clem Clopper wandering around the tree. As they got closer, Becky let go of Ruth's hand and started running towards the base of the tree, where they had left the baby piglet lying in the grass the night before.

Johnny started running right behind her and George, fearing the worst stepped over beside his wife and as George sometimes does, took her hand in his and looked at Ruth and said, "I love you Ruth, I'm so sorry I left that little pig out here last night."

Ruth looked deep into George's eyes, smiled and said "Have a little faith George" then stopped and gave him a big hug. But Becky didn't see her little piggy anywhere. "Clem! Clem Clopper!" Becky shouted "Have you seen our little piggy" Becky asked sternly.

Old Clem has a surprised look on his face, but seemingly understanding Becky. Clem turned towards Mt. Shasta "Whheeeehh-hhh" Clem whinnied, as he tried to rear back, as if to point at the mountain. "Whhheeeehhhhhh" Clem said again.

Johnny laughed, "Silly horse! What the Heck Clem? You tryin' to tell us he's up on Shasta? Good one Clem. Ha, Ha! Crazy old Clem! Really 'pulling our leg'! Ha, Ha Ha!" Johnny said starting to laugh hysterically.

But Becky wasn't laughing "It's not funny Johnny! If Clem thinks he's on the mountain, he could be." That made Johnny start laughing even harder. "Ya Becky, When Pig's Fly! Ha, Ha, Ha! Good One! Ha, Ha, Ha! Get it? When Pigs Fly! Haaa, Ha, Ha, Ha!"

Becky started crying and ran to her mother's arms. "Where is he mommy? Where is our little piggy?"

Ruth embraced her, closely holding and gently rocking her distraught little girl back and forth, with tears in her own eyes. Then, as if to strengthen her young daughter's faith, she pulled back a bit.

Holding Becky's face gently between the palms of her hands, she softly spoke to her, "Honey, you know that God loves and takes care of all of us. You know that, don't you Baby?" she asked again, tears now streaming down both their faces.

"Yes Mommy, don't cry, I know He does." replied Becky between sobs. Ruth pulled Becky's trembling little body close again and hugged her real tight.

"Mommy?" Becky whispered. "Yeah, Baby?" Ruth whispered back.

Becky leaned back in her mother's arms and started to smile as she pulled Mawdy up next to them and looked into her baby blue eyes and said "Mawdy says that "With the Faith to Believe in Love - Life becomes Magic."

Ruth's eyes lit up as she smiled and said, "Oh Mawdy, I love you and you Becky, I love you two." Becky smiled and said, "We love you, too Mommy!"

"Mommy, how come Clem likes you so much more than anybody else?" asked Becky.

"Well Honey, when I was a young girl my Daddy gave him to me for my 16th birthday and it was love at first sight."

"I think Clem is wonderful too" said Becky. That made old Clem perk up and he proudly began strutting his stuff.

Johnny hadn't seen old Clem show this much energy in a long, long time so he decided to take advantage of it. The next time Clem came around close to him, Johnny ran after him and grabbed his mane, then swung himself up on Clem's back.

"Yahoo, Buckskin Buckaroo, Yahoo." Johnny shouted.

But, with that comment, old Clem Clopper must have decided he had about enough of this fun. No sooner had Johnny done his Buckskin Buckaroo holler and old Clem swaggered to a standstill and started eating the grass.

Everyone laughed as Johnny tried to coax old Clem to run again, "Yee Haw, Clem. Getty up, well come on, Getty-up!"

Becky started to laugh and saw a great opportunity to get even with her brother for making fun of her earlier. "Yee haw Johnny" she laughed, "Buckskin Buckaroo!"

Old Clem looked back over his shoulder at Johnny and then started eating grass again. "Looks like his Getty-up and go, done gotty-up and went, huh Mawdy." Becky snickered and everyone laughed once again.

Soon after, George came through the kitchen door and was holding one hand behind his back. When Ruth came over to greet her husband, he presented her with a handful of beautiful wildflowers and a kiss. "I love you Ruthie and supper sure smells good." George was reminded that afternoon just what is truly important the love of his life.

"Oh George, I love you too. Thank you for the flowers, Honey. They're just beautiful. You're so thoughtful." She said smiling up at him sweetly, as she gave her husband a big hug. "I'm going to put these in water while you guys get washed up."

When Ruth went into their bedroom to get her one old glass vase to put her flowers in, such a rush of love washed over her that she clutched her arms around herself and whirled around a time or two.

She looked around the room and her eyes came to rest on the lovely carved wooden music box which sat on their dresser. It was her most cherished possession. George had given her this music box long ago, when they were first courting and the beautifully romantic melody it played was their special song. She placed the flowers into the old vase and lifted the lid of the music box. Ruth closed her eyes, whirled, twirled and swayed as the music Box played "Everything to Me".

Suddenly the magical spell was broken as Johnny came rushing into the room asking "Hey Mom, is dinner ready yet? I'm starving!"

"Ruthie" George interrupted, "let's eat!" It was supper time. So, reality ended her rare fantasy that was "Their Dance".

Soon everyone gathered for dinner. As usual, Ruth said 'the blessing'. George was not a believer, but he respected Ruth's faith and he bowed his head, while she blessed the food. Then everybody was anxious to start eating Ruth's great cooking.

When supper was over, Johnny went out to milk the cow and Becky cleaned off the table. Ruth got the dishwater ready and George went out to make that final round and make sure everything was safe and secure before dark.

That evening, after supper, the full moon was rising and out on the porch old Dawg starts to howl, jaws flapping and ears flying. They all notice the full moon rising, almost rolling up the side of Shasta. Around the fire, the family sat in excited anticipation.

George had promised to share strange stories about Shasta, which he hadn't done in years. Johnny was curled up with Dawg. Becky was hugging Mawdy, while she sat resting her head on Ruth's shoulder. Ruth started giggling as Snuggle Bunny nuzzled close to her ears giving her tuggles. George then turned down the light and sat in front of the fire declaring "It's time."

"I first remember Granddad telling me about the mountain, when I was, oh, I guess about your age Johnny. Yes, in fact it was on a night like tonight. I had seen the night before the strangest of storms." George said. "It was centered over the top of Shasta and it seemed to be drawn there. There was all kinds of lightning and thunder, but, no other clouds in the sky. Ya know, Granddaddy used to tell stories he heard from others about flying horses and such. He never much believed them though."

As Becky giggled, Ruth smiled, "Oh George, now really honey!" she said laughing at his fantasy. George ignored the jeering from his girls. He continued his story telling until it was time for bed. As Ruth is tucking in Becky she asks "Mommy, do you believe our little piggy is up with God?"

Ruth answers, "Of Course I do." Johnny asks, "Why doesn't dad believe in faith?" Ruth comfortingly says, "Your dad is a very good man, but not a believer."

Becky asks, "Mawdy wants to know why not?"

"Well Mawdy", Ruth says "His heart has not yet been touched by God, but someday he will believe. Always remember Mawdy "With the Faith to Believe in Love ~ Life becomes Magic!".

With that Becky and Mawdy said their prayers. Johnny said his and pondered the strange storm stories. Snuggle Bunny can't stay in, so Ruth puts him out on the front porch. Then George & Ruth went off to sleep. The Bennett's long day was finally over.

Snuggle Bunny began to wander through the barnyard thinking about what he had just heard. He then scampered across the pasture to large oak tree on the hill, where he knew he could find his old friend Clem Clopper. Clem was trying to sleep and Snuggle got up close to him and tried to wake him up but couldn't. Snuggle tried shaking him and even pulled on one of his whiskers. Finally, he went over to Clem's face and slowly opened his eyelids and said, "Clem are you awake?"

As Old Clem's eye opened, he focused in on Snuggles eyes only inches from his face and it must have startled him because Clem lunged to his feet instantly, which sent Snuggle rolling head over heels backwards across the grass.

When he regained his composer, Snuggles proceeded to tell Clem about the stories he had heard back at the house. Clem listened for a while and then interrupted Snuggle Bunny. "Kinda reminds me of the stories great granddaddy Clopper used to tell."

Looking deep into Snuggle Bunny's eyes, Clem continued, "When I was just a little 'Clip-Clopper', I remember great granddaddy Clopper telling me about the mighty Pegasus and magical Unicorn, who would come to this very pasture and visit the "Presence". Once they even talked to granddaddy Clopper and told him to always believe in the Presence and all that he has seen. But, no one ever believed great granddaddy Clopper's stories. In fact, most still don't believe the stories that have been passed on through the generations. I was never sure that I did, that is until last night!"

Snuggle Bunny looked at Clem kinda confused like and asked "What do you mean?

"Well Snuggle, remember that poor little runt pig that no one can find." Clem paused and Snuggle said "Ya, the one that died and went to be with God?!" Clem looked him straight in the eye with his most serious look, which is hard for Clem, and said "Saved Snuggle Bunny! Saved! Not dead! Saved!!"

Snuggle was obviously confused. Even a little scared. He had never seen Clem so serious. "W-what do you mean s-s-saved. Everyone thought he was --- You know d-d-dead." Clem replied "Saved! Not dead!"

Snuggle Bunny was obviously confused, so Clem went on to explain to the little guy what he had seen. When Clem had finished his fantastic story, Snuggle looked up at him and innocently asked "You think that runt pig will ever come back Clem?"

Clem thought about it a minute and then gazed high above the old tree and up at the ancient volcano Shasta. As Clem and Snuggle Bunny looked on, the full moon was shining brightly between the East Peak and the large west crater, casting an almost mystical glow on Mt. Shasta and across the valley below.

"Yep, great granddaddy Clopper was right Snuggles and somehow I don't think we've seen the last of that pig." Snuggle yawns a cute little tuggle yawn and that makes old Clem Clopper yawn a big old barnyard yawn. They both decide that it's time to 'hit the hay'.

Clem takes Snuggle Bunny back to the house by Becky's window. Snuggle climbs onto Clem's nose and gets lifted through the window. Clem just smiled and wandered off back towards the barn. As he walked, Clem took one last look at the full moon above Shasta.

Then old Clem said "Whhheeeehhhhh" almost as if howling at the moon. Clem smiled and wandered back to the pasture near the ancient oak and falls fast asleep.

Later that night a single black cloud appears on the horizon to the south. In a short period of time, the thunderstorm travels straight to the peak of Shasta, growing steadily in intensity, yet still a single storm cloud, just as in the strange storm stories told earlier that night.

Now high above Shasta, the full moon seemed to begin to turn a very faint, but distinct blue. As the storm settles in the pass between the east peak and the west crater, a mystical blue light begins to shine from within the storm. It grows and grows in intensity until it is almost a brilliant white light. Then, with a single bolt of blue lightning crackling from deep within the storm and striking near the old cave, the light begins to vanish.

As the strange storm mysteriously traveled quickly to the east, fading into the night, the mighty roar of Rintrah echoed from the cliff above the cave, where the blue lightning had struck. "Rroooaaarrrrr!"

As spring turns into summer back in Shasta Valley, life continues as usual for the Bennett's. George and Ruth teach their children about faith, hope, love, family, forgiveness and lessons about right, wrong and the ways of the world through various chores and day to day family life. Although all seems swell for the family, the chilling wind marks the coming of fall and as foretold, the impending evil brews in the depths of Shasta's dark crater: the evil RATHVAR, nemesis to all love and light, begins his return.

Meanwhile, home in Elysium, Pigasus has grown to be a fine looking young pig as have his magnificent rainbow colored wings. He now knows he is somehow "special", but still has no idea the significance of his destiny. Unisus is always by his side, teaching him about faith, hope, love, family, forgiveness and lessons about right, wrong and the ways of the world. Always encouraging him to prepare for his fate, which she knows draws near.

Although the young Pigasus is adolescently awkward and naive, Unisus knows he must gain courage and wisdom to confront the evil darkness of Rathvar. But what even Unisus does not realize is ultimately, only by a leap of faith, can the battle for evermore be won.

Summer quickly passed and on the night before the full harvest moon, Unicorn, Pegasus, Unisus & Pigasus returned from Elysium, majestically flying from down beneath the east peak towards Shasta valley. As they neared the old oak, we see the Bennett family fast asleep and so is old Clem, snoring loudly in the pasture.

Unisus landed first and Unicorn gracefully landed beside her. As the mighty Pegasus began to land, we see Pigasus awkwardly trying to hold on to Pegasus's neck, while sitting streamlined between his mighty wings. Pigasus has clearly grown into a plump adolescent pig.

As Pegasus landed, Pigasus bounced atop his back, his big belly making Pegasus's back bow a little. Pegasus spread his wing down to the grass for Pigasus to get off, but instead of sliding off gracefully, he rolled, bounced and landed flat on his belly. Starring up at Unisus, Unicorn, Pegasus and the old oak tree, they all laughed, as Pigasus humbly smiled back.

Then the brilliant blue light and swirling gold dust of the Presence appears in the ancient oak tree. Pigasus is fascinated as he watched Unicorn & Pegasus approach the Presence. They stood face to face, then turned toward the Presence, bowed gracefully, and reared back on their hind legs as two mighty bolts of blue lightning struck each of them. Once again touched by the Presence, Unicorn & Pegasus leapt side by side, vanishing into His loving light.

There is a moment of silence. "W-where'd they go Unisus. They just disappeared." Pigasus asked.

"They went to visit the one they love the most and share their love with him." Unisus said in her softest loving voice.

Unisus then began to walk towards the Presence and she almost stumbled over the slightly frightened, but curious pig. She stopped for a moment and looked down at Pigasus, who was huddled close to her. "Pigasus, you must wait here while I too again proclaim my love and commitment to the Loving Light of the – Presence."

Pigasus protested "But Unisus, I'm scared. What's going on? Where did Unicorn and Pegasus go? Are they all right? I wanna go!"

"Pigasus, they are with the Presence. They love him and have gone to visit with him." Unisus said quietly. Pigasus looked up at Unisus, somewhat relieved and calmer but, somehow confused. "But, Unisus, the Presence is right there in the tree. They didn't have to leave."

Unisus looked at Pigasus, whose sincere look of innocence made her realize that he really didn't understand, so she continued to explain. "That is the loving light of the Presence, Pigasus. But The Presence is everywhere. Don't you remember Pigasus?"

Pigasus was obviously becoming overwhelmed with all this, but he didn't really want to admit it. "You mean Unicorn and Pegasus actually get to go see the Presence."

"Yes, they do Pigasus." Unisus replied. "They cherish this time with the Presence. They have been with him since their beginning."

With that pleasant thought he began to see the faint image of Unicorn and Pegasus walking towards the beautiful Unisus. A smile began to grow across his face. As they slowly emerged from within the loving light of the Presence, Pigasus began running towards them.

They continued walking until they stood facing the elated Pigasus, who came clumsily to a halt before running into the mighty Pegasus. There they all stood, poised in front of the sacred oak with the brilliant light of the Presence and the full blue moon reflected in the eyes of Pigasus.

The mighty Pegasus looked deep into the eyes of Pigasus and began to speak, "Since the days of future passed has this day been foretold and the fate of Elysium is near. You, Pigasus were chosen from all others. The outcast. The special one, chosen to do battle against the Evil Rathvar. The time of your fate is near. You will face the blackness of the darkness and the deceptions of doubt. You will question all that is and be tempted not to believe in the loving light of the Presence."

Pigasus looked up at Pegasus and Unicorn with eyes as big as the moon, "But, I Believe! I love the Presence. I could never stop believing in Him." he said shakily. Unicorn looked at Pigasus with love and reassurance, "Of course you love him, but the power of evil is strong. Rathvar will try to deceive your heart Pigasus. You must always hold on to all that is true and search your heart for the truth, the light and love of the Presence. It is your fate."

Pegasus again spoke, "The choice will be yours my son, you will know, if when the blackness of the darkness surrounds you, you find the faith to believe in all that you know to be true in your heart. Love will win!"

Pegasus had never called Pigasus son and a tear appeared in the eyes of Pigasus, as he proudly assured Pegasus and Unicorn that he would always believe. A reflection of the Presence was in his eye. He turned to the sacred oak, "I Believe!" proudly proclaiming his acceptance of his fate, and then awkwardly kneeled in front of the Presence. Then the Presence spoke, "Pigasus! The future is now past. Your time to meet your fate is near. Pigasus, you must 'find the faith to believe' and you must confront the evil Rathvar in the Battle for Evermore."

Pigasus prepares himself in front of the Presence and rears back in expectation of being struck with the mark of Elysium. He falls over backwards and clumsily starts to get back up. As he struggles to his feet Unicorn and Pegasus walk on either side of him and facing him rear back. As they do, the Presence strikes Pigasus with a brilliant bolt of blue lightning, just as he had struck Unisus earlier and creates the heart shaped mark of Elysium.

The once outcast piglet left to die now had the Heart of Elysium permanently on his rump. "Wow!" Pigasus said in amazement. "I have a Heart on my butt." As he looked over his shoulder shaking his butt proudly up in the air with his pig tail emulating little circles.

"Pigasus!" Unisus said trying not to laugh, "The Presence -- "she said to him to remind him his butt wasn't that special, and he should focus back on the Presence.

Pigasus caught with his tail high in the air, suddenly realized he was shaking his butt at everyone and blushed with embarrassment, while also trying not to laugh. He again faced the Presence standing tall and proud.

This event signified Pigasus has come of age and brings to bear the beginning of the days of future passed and the foretold start of his quest to battle the evil Rathvar, which would soon determine the fate of all Elysium.

Unicorn, Pegasus, Unisus and Pigasus remained focused on the loving light of the Presence. Still watching in amazement near them is old Clem Clopper. Behind the pasture, towering above them in the background is the ancient volcano Shasta with the full moon shining high above.

A dumbfounded Pigasus standing before the Presence, turns slowly towards Pegasus and then to Unicorn. Then Pegasus leaned down and looked deep into the eyes of Pigasus saying, "Remember all you have seen and all you have learned, for your future is our fate."

Pigasus didn't understand and looked over at Unicorn who simply said, "Follow your heart Pigasus, it will never betray you."

With those remarks, they turned towards the Presence, reared back and vaulted into the night sky, flying towards Mt. Shasta. As Pigasus watched in the disbelief that they would just leave him, Unisus walked over towards him and gave him a comforting nuzzle across his cheek. As she did, a small tear rolled from the eye of Pigasus and trickled onto her nose.

"Where are they going Unisus? Why are they leaving? Are they coming back?" Pigasus was asking with a definite note of sadness in his voice.

Unisus softly replied, "They are going to Elysium to be with the Presence. They will not return until your quest is complete, and Elysium is forever again."

Pigasus could not believe his ears, "Never coming back?"

Unisus tried to comfort Pigasus. "They will always be in your heart Pigasus, always remember them and they will always be with you."

Somehow that made sense to Pigasus and did seem to make him feel a little better. Then he began to sense that Unisus too would be leaving. "Your leaving too aren't you."

Unisus looked deep into the eyes of Pigasus. "You see Pigasus; your heart knows you must stay. I will be back if it is the will of the Presence. Always remember Pigasus, believe in all you know and follow your heart. We are all always in your heart."

With those words, she again nuzzled her nose against the now tear covered cheeks of Pigasus and then vaulted high into the night sky towards Shasta. Pigasus is left standing in front of the Presence.

He sighs, then notices the Presence fading and appearing again, high atop the ancient volcano Shasta. He looks on in amazement, as he sees the faint images of Unicorn, Pegasus and Unisus approaching the pass between the once twin peaks of the mystical Shasta.

As the loving light of the Presence became brighter & brighter, Pigasus could see the lights of Elysium began to illuminate the night sky high above Mt. Shasta. "WOW" he said out loud to himself "That's Awesome!"

But, as the light of the Presence faded, Pigasus quickly realized he was now truly alone for the first time ever. He was scared and confused. As he fell asleep under the old oak, he wondered how he could ever be brave enough to confront the evil Rathvar, let alone do battle with him. The situation seemed hopeless.

Small tears began to roll down his cheeks, as Pigasus closed his eyes and cried himself to sleep sarcastically whispering to himself, "Sweet Dreams". As soon as he fell asleep, we see a smile appear on his face. Pigasus actually begins having sweet dreams about his most wonderful and magical days growing up in the paradise Elysium.

But as it was foretold; somewhere, something evil brews and from the depths of the crater on the ancient volcano Shasta, where the Blackness of the Darkness had been cast out 10 millenniums ago. The evil Rathvar begins his return.

The following day Clem Clopper awoke to see Snuggle Bunny heading towards him to say good morning, like he would do on most mornings. But, Snuggle sees something under the tree and says, "What the heck?" He runs over toward Pigasus and yells to Clem to come and join him.

As Clem swaggers over, Snuggle focuses his attention on the sleeping pig, which is sort of snoring funny?!!! Snuggle Bunny tries shaking him and telling the pig to wake up. Then he notices the rainbow wings on the pig's back and he again says, "What the heck?"

Snuggle yells to Clem, "Hey, this pig has wings?!" Then he turns back to investigating the strange new arrival and in the excitement of his discovery gives the pig a 'Tha-Pah', a harmless bunny kick.

Snuggle looked confused, "Hey Clem, he didn't move." He carefully walk around Pigasus until he was sure this pig was no monster. About then, Pigasus grunted and sighed, which startled Snuggle and he jumped back. That made old Clem start laughing. They both began to laugh at each other and this strange looking pig. A pig with wings.

Snuggle approached Pigasus again and tried to wake him. He shouted and gently kicked him 'Tha-Pah'. But it didn't wake the pig. Then Snuggle realized something very peculiar, "Clem, this pig has a heart shaped nose!" Finally, he got very close to Pigasus's face and slowly raised one of his eyelids. "Hello?" Snuggle asked staring him eye to eye.

Pigasus wakes up blurry eyed, realizes Snuggle, who just kicked him, is just inches from his face. They stare at each other for a moment and then Pigasus realizes he's in a strange new place and it really scares him. Pigasus abruptly jumped to his feet scarring the carrots out of Snuggle Bunny, which made Clem break out in laughter.

He'd never seen a rabbit before and was sure he must be some kind of monster. "Help, Unisus help! MONSTER!!" Pigasus jumped up and started running from Snuggle yelling "Shoo-stay away -Shoo!"

Pigasus ran in circles and tried to use his wings. But he tumbled & rolled skidding right back to Snuggle Bunny's feet. His nose in the dirt, Pigasus smiled, looked up and proudly shared, "Hi, I'm Pigasus!"

They all quickly became the best of friends and even though Pigasus didn't remember, both Snuggle Bunny and Clem knew this was the same runt piglet that vanished from the pasture back in the springtime.

It wasn't long before Johnny, Becky and Mawdy discovered Pigasus. Becky immediately knew he was the same pig and he had wings! "Look Mawdy. What beautiful wings".

All three looked at Pigasus and he looked back at them. In his eyes they saw a reflection of the light of Elysium. When it faded Johnny and Becky looked at each other and then Becky heard Pigasus speak, "Hi! I'm Pigasus."

Becky introduced herself and Mawdy. "Why hello Mr. Pigasus! My name is Becky; this is Mawdy, my brother Johnny and Dawg. Very nice to meet you sir", she said politely. "Mawdy, look! He has a heart shaped nose, just like --"Becky reached out and touched his nose and Pigasus smiled, just as he had done as the little runt piglet and Becky's eyes lit up and she got the biggest smile - "It's you! My little piggy, you've come home!"

Then Becky realizes this is NOT make believe, "Pigasus, you can talk!

Clem said, "Of course he can talk." Then Clem realized he could understand Becky, but not Johnny. They all figured it must be some kind of magic or something. Johnny just figured they were all a little nuts.

Pigasus started to explain that he was from Elysium, a most wondrous place, where everything was beautiful. He told them about Unicorn, Pegasus, Unisus and the mighty Rintrah!

But Johnny couldn't see the wings and was clearly frustrated with all this make believe nonsense. Becky just laughed, as they all headed back to the house to share their wonderful discovery. It wasn't easy, but Ruth convinced George, who also thought this was all nonsense, to reluctantly allow 'The Pig' to stay.

Johnny wasted no time, "To the Scuttlebutt" he shouted. He picked up Snuggle Bunny and pushed Pigasus out the door towards the pond. "Aarrgh-maties! All aboard the pirate ship 'Scuttlebutt'", an old wood raft with a makeshift flagpole and whitewashed skull & crossbones flying high.

They bravely sailed into the middle of the pond. But the evil Rathvar appeared in the depths of the water creating a wicked whirlpool. As they began to spin, Pigasus looked into the water and saw his reflection, but his wings were GONE!

"My Wings! Where are my WINGS!", Pigasus screamed in panic.

But it was an evil illusion created by Rathvar. The raft spun faster & faster. Then Pigasus leaned over the edge too far! SPLASH! It was the wreck of the Scuttlebutt.

As they all fell overboard, the wicked whirlpool vanished. Johnny & Snuggle Bunny were clearly frustrated with the 'crazy pig'. Embarrassed, Pigasus muttered, "My wings! I still have my wings". Snuggle Bunny climbed up on Pigasus's belly, soaking wet, as Pigasus used his wings to swim towards shore.

Johnny laughed, "Dumb Pig! Chasing your tail on a pirate ship! You Wrecked the Scuttle Butt! Good thing for us pigs float!" Thankfully they all made it safely to shore.

Ruth & Becky watched, laughing as they came towards the house. "Mawdy" Becky yelled "It's Time for Tea!" Ruth smiled and handed Becky a fresh plate of Chocolate Chip cookies, Clem's favorite!

Becky & Mawdy rushed out back and coaxed Old Clem, Snuggle Bunny & Pigasus to "Join them for tea", setting cookies around the table out back. She then placed empty teacups and poured them all make believe tea. Becky made them wait though until everything was ready. "OK, you may begin." Becky said as she picked up her cup of tea and very realistically took an imaginary sip.

Pigasus and Snuggle Bunny, wanting to do everything just right, took Becky's lead and prepared to drink their tea. Since they couldn't pick up their cups, Snuggle Bunny hesitantly stuck his nose into his cup a little way, then a little further and further until he was nearly standing on his head trying to get a taste of the tea that wasn't there.

Pigasus had watched Snuggles struggle for a minute and then decided to try his own luck, or lack of it, as it turned out. He soon found that fitting a big pig snout into a very small cup is a difficult task. He tried first straight on, then to one side and then the other but nothing seemed to work. Pigasus and Snuggle both realized there was no tea and wanted to know what happened to the tea.

"It's pretend tea, Silly" said Becky. "You have to believe it's real."

"How can you make believe it's real if there's nothing there" asked Snuggle.

Becky tried to explain "It's like God. You can't see Him, but if you believe He's real, then He is real. It's the same with tea!"

Pigasus thought about it and said, "Yeah, just like the Presence. I understand now."

Becky and Snuggle Bunny both looked at him kinda funny because they didn't know what he was talking about. "Can we have a cookie now?" Pigasus asked.

But Rathvar again appeared, his powers growing ever stronger. Up on the mountain a dark storm was brewing. A bolt of lightning crackled through the sky and the rumbling sound of thunder filled the air. Then a strong cold wind began to blow and disrupt the tea party.

In the wind, we hear Rathvar whispering "Believe, believe in the darkness." Then we see a large snake appear in the grass, clearly an illusion created by the evil Rathvar, as it slowly slithers towards Becky. The wind is still blowing, but now it's Rathvar's voice whispering from the snake, "Believe! Believe in the darkness."

It seemed as though everyone heard the voice in the cold wind. Even Mawdy seemed to get shivers of eerie fear. They look at one another very apprehensively. The slithering snake still silently approaching Becky. Just before it reached her, Clem saw it and leaped over the table sending everything flying and began awkwardly stomping on 'the snake'.

Old Clem hopped, stomped and trampled up and down and sideways. When he finally stopped all that remained of that snake was a large broken up branch from the tree. They all started laughing at Clem, as the illusion of the snake vanished and all that remained was just a twig. Clem stopped stomping and looking a little embarrassed, he began laughing at himself, but in his heart Clem new something was wrong.

"WOW!" Snuggle exclaimed. "What was that Clem? The Clopper Hopper or the Kaddidle Hopper", he said starting to laugh at old Clem's "Dancing". They all looked down at the broken branch. They all decided they thought they had seen a snake---they thought.

"It was Rathvar" Pigasus said. "He was here. I heard his voice in the wind." They all agreed they had heard the voice. "Pegasus always told me, when your scared of something dark to believe in the light. That light always shines through the darkness. You just have to have the faith to believe. Yep! With the Faith to Believe in Love — Life becomes Magic!"

"Oh, I believe, Pigasus, I believe!" Becky said sincerely. "Thank you, Clem, thank you for saving me." Becky gave Clem a big old hug. Then thought to herself and asked, "Mawdy, what's a Pegasus?"

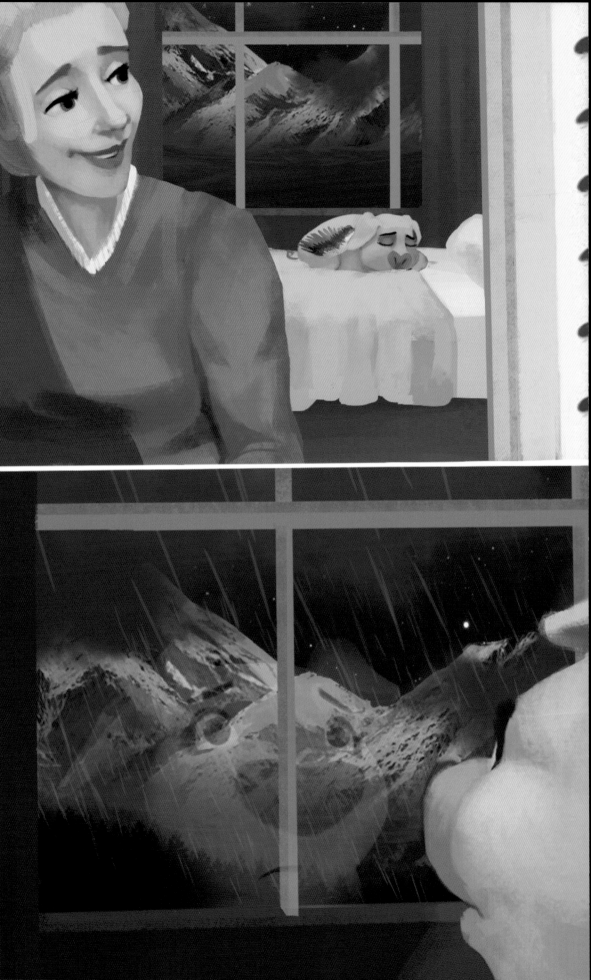

As bedtime approached, all the thunder and lightning from the strange storm above Shasta was really starting to scare Becky & Mawdy. So, after Ruth tucked them in and shared their prayers, she sat on the edge of Becky's bed and quietly began to sing a song that had been sung to her by her mother and thus passed down through the generations. Pigasus and Snuggle Bunny had never heard the lullaby and they all got very quiet as Ruth began to sing.

"All you need is Faith, Hope, Love, Family and a Rainbows & Roses Lullaby." She then continued to "Hum" the melodic melody & chorus of the beautiful "Rainbows & Roses Lullaby". It was Becky and Mawdy's very favorite song in the whole world! But, almost before Ruth can finish the first chorus, they are all fast asleep. All tuggled and cuddled in for the night and soon everyone was fast asleep.

High above the valley Shasta we see all of the snow rapidly melt away leaving the mountain barren. The dark clouds continue to build over the peaks and spread across the sky and a dark bolt of black lightning struck the depths of the crater. It was a mighty bolt that shook the once towering west peak of Shasta. The roar of the thunder awoke Pigasus and he somehow knew it was the evil Rathvar.

Pigasus gets up and looks out the window. Another mighty bolt of black lightning struck, but this time it struck the east peak of the ancient volcano. Pigasus stared up at the growing storm and we see it reflected in his eyes.

He then heard a roar, a mighty roar "Rooaarrr!" from somewhere atop Shasta. Pigasus took comfort in knowing he had just heard the mighty Rintrah, guarding the cliff between the twin peaks of Elysium.

But, as a very strong cold wind blows through the land, Pigasus hears in a loud and evil whisper, "I've returned. I, Rathvar, have returned." It was the evil Rathvar, bringing with him the Blackness of his Darkness.

Later that night Pigasus saw Unisus returning to Shasta valley, flying and galloping gracefully through the night sky. She lands next to the old oak, where Clem Clopper is sleeping. Pigasus, was so excited he jumped out of the window and ran to Unisus, maybe as fast as he had ever run! "Unisus! I've missed you so much!" he said, as he crossed the bridge and started up the hill, where she stood looking sternly back at him.

Just as he got close, Pigasus was so excited, he didn't see old Clem's hoof. Pigasus tripped over it, tumbling and rolling to a pigstop right at the feet of Unisus. Old Clem kinda grunted, snorted and went right on snoring.

Pigasus looked up smiling, knowing his Pigstop always made everyone laugh but Unisus had a very serious look in her eyes. "Unisus! I'm so happy to see you." Pigasus said, as he sat up and smiled at her.

Unisus looked down and in a most serious voice said, "Pigasus, the time of darkness is near. We must have a heart to heart talk." Pigasus, sat looking up at Unisus realizing the urgency of her visit, but not the importance of what she was about to say. Unisus starts by reminding him of Elysium, Unicorn & Pegasus and their love for him. Then with a very serious tone reminded him of his fate. That soon he must confront the evil Rathvar.

"Remember! You must find the faith to believe." Unisus paused "I Love you Pigasus." Then she leapt into the night sky and gracefully galloped towards Mt. Shasta leaving a trail of magical golden dust behind her. Pigasus was stunned that she left him.

As he watched her fade into the night sky, the Black Lightning of Rathvar flashed on the mountain. As he slowly laid down in the grass, he heard a voice whispering across the wind, "It is I, Rathvar! I have returned." This clearly scared Pigasus! Thankfully old Clem Clopper was lying nearby, snoring loudly and seeing how funny he looked, Pigasus smiled and was soon fast asleep.

But, above the west crater of Shasta, the blackness of the darkness grew. As foretold, the evil Rathvar had indeed returned.

The next morning the storm has passed to a beautiful new day. As the first dawns light peeked over Shasta, the sunlight quickly reached the pasture where Pigasus was sleeping and strangely lit up his face. He got a big smile and snuggled back into the grass feeling the warmth of the new day's sunlight.

The dawn's light also struck the face of Snuggle Bunny and strangely lit up his face. He got a big smile, opened his eyes and quickly realized Pigasus was gone! He immediately hopped up onto the windowsill looking out towards the pasture for him. Sure, enough there sleeping next to old Clem Copper was Pigasus. Snuggle Bunny smiled and as it were any other morning, hopped out the window and went bouncing across the bridge towards them.

As he got close, Snuggle Bunny couldn't believe what he saw flying out of the rising sun. It was the beautiful Unisus flying towards the ranch, galloping gracefully through the sky towards him leaving a trail of magical golden dust. This got Snuggles very excited and his back foot started thumping the ground and his heart started twitterpatting! Clearly this was Bunny Love. He was so excited he hopped right onto the back of Pigasus, where his foot kept right on thumping.

"Pigasus, wake up! It's Unisus! She's here. Pigasus! Pigasus! Wake Up!" he said hopping off his back and now kicking Pigasus in the rump! "Tha-Pah! Tha-Pah! Wake Up!". Snuggle couldn't believe how slow Pigasus was moving.

"What? Huh? Unisus?" Pigasus said opening one eye to see Snuggles eye starring right back at him! This startled Pigasus! As he jumped up, it sent Snuggle Bunny bouncing back on his tail. Pigasus tried to run, but he tripped on old Clem's hoof and went rolling, tumbling and bouncing across the grass. Then skidded to a stop at the feet of Unisus in perfect 'Pigstop' fashion.

Pigasus looked up at Unisus who was trying to hide a smile. "Oops, I kind of goofed."

Unisus smiled and told Pigasus how happy she was to see him and then she looked behind him. Pigasus turned and saw old Clem Clopper laughing at him and then he saw Snuggle Bunny. He wasn't laughing. He had a very strange look on his face, obviously enchanted by the beautiful Unisus.

"Hey, Snuggle, what's the matter with you?" Pigasus asked innocently.

Clem was still laughing, as he swaggered past Snuggle, who was still starring at Unisus. "Why he's in Bunny Love! Snuggles is twitterpatted!"

That snapped him out of his trance. "Love, heck no, not me, not Snuggle Bunny." he said defiantly. He then looked back at Unisus and smiled. Everyone just laughed.

Pigasus told her how happy he was to see her but wanted to know why she had come back so soon. Unisus began to explain. "Rathvar has returned, Pigasus, and he is near." She looked up at the barren Shasta.

Pigasus answered her. "I heard him too Unisus. He tried to hurt my friends. I heard him last night and knew it was him that caused that terrible storm last night. I was scared for a while. Then I heard Rintrah! I'm sure it was him and I knew he would protect us."

Pigasus seemed confident that everything would be O.K. since the mighty Rintrah was near. Then Unisus spoke, "He cannot protect you Pigasus, none of us can. It is destiny that brought us together and it is fate that brings me here today. The time is near Pigasus. It is your fate that you confront the evil Rathvar."

They all looked very concerned and Pigasus became frightened. "I'm scared Unisus. How can I fight Rathvar? Oh, I don't know what to do." He sunk his snout down close to the ground almost ashamed at his fear.

"You must believe Pigasus. Believe in the light of the Presence and the love in your heart. Believe, Pigasus. Then all things will come to pass as they should be." With those words she turned and leaped into the air and flew back towards the volcano Shasta.

"Unisus wait!" Pigasus seemed almost desperate. "I must find her Snuggle; I have to talk to her." He then started running across the pasture and never looked back. Snuggle Bunny started to run after him, but, old Clem Clopper was too old to go chasing after Unisus, not to mention he was still sleeping and snoring loudly.

They quickly decided they were going to climb Mt. Shasta to look for Unisus and investigate the strange storm, still raging, but only right above the crater. It took almost all day. Finally, they had reached the high mountain pass between the towering peaks of Shasta.

"Unisus! Unisus!" Pigasus called and called. She was not to be found. Eventually, they found themselves at the base of a cliff beneath the crater. There standing in front of a cave, a dark cave, Pigasus wondered if Unisus could be inside. "Unisus? Are you in there Unisus?"

Then, from within the cave, a strong cold wind blew, and we hear the voice of Rathvar, but it sounds like Unisus. "Pigasus, help me Pigasus. I'm here in the darkness." Pigasus knew the voice sounded strange but, he had to find Unisus, so he ventured into the cave.

Snuggle is confused. He seemed sure that wasn't Unisus. "Pigasus wait. Where are you going? It's dark in there Pigasus, come back."

Pigasus looked back for a moment and shook his head no. "I must find Unisus, I must." He then heard the tainted voice of Unisus again. Deeper into the darkness he went.

"Is this a short cut? Oh-Oh, wait for me." With that Snuggle hopped quickly into the cave and right under Pigasus, he had to dodge his belly of course. They crept slowly following the fading voice "Help me Pigasus." Rathvar drew them further and further away from the light and into the darkness.

As they did, the voice of Unisus stopped. All became very quiet and still. It was an eerie feeling and they both began to realize they too were lost in the blackness of the darkness. From the depths of the cave they began to see a black void. It was something, but nothing. It grew, rapidly filling the cave. "I'm sca-sca-scared." Snuggle said shakily.

A large translucent form appeared in the blackness. Suddenly a bolt of black lightning crackled through the darkness and rocked the cave. Then ominous red eyes appeared in the blackness of the darkness scaring Snuggle Bunny. He quickly hopped up on Pigasus's back. As the eerie eyes grew larger and larger, they saw a wickedly evil smile.

The cave began to rumble and shake. They heard a voice, "Yes, it is I, Rathvar!" That really scared them and Pigasus immediately turned and ran out of the cave, actually flying for the first time. Pigasus awkwardly flew back towards the pasture with Snuggle Bunny holding onto Pigasus's ears for dear life.

Clem was standing near the oak in the pasture and saw Pigasus and Snuggle Bunny flying out of control towards him. Snuggle hears Pigasus saying "1-2, 1-2" and starts to laugh.

Then Snuggle realizes that maybe Pigasus really doesn't know how to fly and they really might crash. So, he starts yelling into Pigasus's ear in a panic. "No Pigasus not 1-2, 1-2. Think 2-2, 2-2 both wings at the same time Pigasus."

Pigasus heard him and started counting "2-2, 2-2." It was starting to work, but he was going too fast and was surely going to crash. "Lookout Clem, I can't land."

He quickly changed his mind and started thinking about how to flap his wings "1-2, 1-2" which sent them fluttering through the air and tumbling towards the pasture.

Clem now realized the inevitable. Pigasus was going to crash again and was heading straight for him. "Oh no, not again."

Snuggle Bunny then crouched really low and pleaded. "No Pigasus! Not the Pigstop flop. Noooo!"

They bounced, rolled and ended in a pigstop at Clem's feet. Pigasus humbly looked up and smiled, as Snuggle Bunny was still clutching to Pigasus's ears in shock. Pigasus then stood up and as he started to tell old Clem his amazing story, Snuggle Bunny ran as fast as he could towards the safety of the Bennett's house.

But Rathvar is just getting started and the blackness of his darkness grows with the strange storm again forming above Shasta. It was soon supper time. They all sat down at the dinner table, but before Ruth could even say grace, Becky began quizzing her father. "Daddy Pigasus Flew and saved Snuggles from the evil Rathvar and why is that scary storm getting so big and who's Rathvar and--."

Ruth interrupts "Rebecca Lynn." she said politely, "Please wait until after you've had your supper for such tales of adventure."

Becky then tried to explain. "No Mommy, it's true. Snuggle Bunny told us and Pigasus flew down from the mountain and saved bunny and everything."

Then the sound of thunder is heard rumbling off in the distance. George comments "Sounds like there's a thunderstorm a brewin' Ruthie."

"No, it's Rathvar." Becky interrupted. With that another roar of thunder is heard and a strange darkness appeared in the eyes of George, "Enough of this foolish fantasy!" he shouted angrily. "Now not another word." The darkness of Rathvar had touched George's heart. Becky and Mawdy both cringed in disbelief. "Oh, Daddy!" she said with tears welling up in her eyes.

As they all quietly finished supper, the sound of thunder again rumbled through the valley. It was soon time for bed and as they headed off to bed, Becky softly asked her Daddy for a kiss goodnight. But George was still angry and insisted on not giving any kids, who had more time for foolish fantasy than supper, a good night kiss. Becky was truly sad and with a tear in her eye ran for bed. Ruth looked at George "Oh George, how could you!" she said almost scolding him as she followed Becky into her bedroom.

As Becky begins to pray, she hears the thunder crash and a strong wind blew through the bedroom window. "Believe in the darkness," whispered through the wind. They did not seem to hear the evil Rathvar, who so desperately wanted them not to pray.

We then see a light begin to shine in the far ceiling corner of the room. It is clearly the loving light of the Presence, who has come to hear Becky's prayer. The warmth of the Presence filled the room. "God, thank you for loving us and keeping us safe. Please be nice to Daddy. Daddy loves us. Thank you for bringing Pigasus back and please keep him safe. I believe in you." The light of the Presence seemed to glow brighter in the love Becky expressed and we could see the reflection of it in Becky's eyes.

"Mommy why is Daddy so angry with us. Did we do something wrong?" wondered Becky.

"Of course, you didn't." Ruth said in a quiet comforting voice. She then tries to explain to them that their father doesn't mean to be so harsh. He works very hard and has no time for foolishness after a hard day. "He is a good man Becky and he loves you all very much."

"Mommy how come Daddy never prays with us, doesn't he believe in God?" Becky asked with the innocence only a child can have. "Johnny believes, Mawdy believes and you believe in God, doesn't Daddy?"

"No, he doesn't" confessed Ruth. "But, if he would only open his heart, I'm sure he would."

The light of the Presence then seemed to grow and lit up the entire room. "Could we pray for Daddy, Mommy? I'm sure God loves him. Dear God, Mommy says my Daddy is a good man and I love him very, very much. Please tell Daddy you love him."

Ruth and Johnny both had a small tear in their eye as Becky innocently smiled, hugged Mawdy and jumped into bed. Becky saw the tear in their eye and said, "It's all right! God heard me." Again, we see the reflection of the Presence in Becky's eyes and watch it fade from the room. Ruth tucked them both in and said goodnight.

As the light of the Presence faded the storm on the mountain grew and grew. The dark clouds now covered the ancient volcano Shasta and thunder filled the air as black lightning arched throughout the darkness. There was a cold wind blowing hard through the valley and night grew very, very dark.

In the house, everyone was fast asleep, except for Becky, who sleeps right next to the window. She is awake and very frightened from the scary storm. "I'm scared Mawdy. Are you scared? Oh, Mawdy I wish you could talk to me like Pigasus can. I'm so scared."

Becky looks out the window and sees black lightning strike the east peak of Shasta and she holds Mawdy close. "Oh Mawdy." But, before Becky & Mawdy could fall asleep, the lightning flashed, and the exploding thunder continued to scare them very much.

Just when she thought the storm could get no worse, Becky noticed a strange light over the mountains to the east. The light grew brighter and brighter. She knew it couldn't be the sun be-cause it wasn't morning. "Look Mawdy, something wonderful is happening!"

Becky knew it couldn't be the moon because the light was different. It was blue. She kneeled up on the bed and watched the angry storm fade, as the blue light got brighter and brighter. She then heard a thunderous roar from the top of Shasta. "Rooaarrr!"

It was the mighty Rintrah. As he roared again, Becky & Mawdy saw the full moon rise above the mountains. It seemed to roll up the side of the ancient volcano and come to rest just above the East peak and it was blue. Becky was amazed, "Look Mawdy! It's BLUE! The full moon is actually BLUE!"

Out in the pasture, we see Clem Clopper, Snuggle Bunny and Pigasus all nestled down close to one another under the shelter of the sacred oak. Then Pigasus stood up looking up towards Mt. Shasta and proclaimed, "It's the Return of the Blue Moon! Look! It's the Lights of Elysium!"

Clem and Snuggle Bunny stood up next to Pigasus now also watching this most spectacular sight. "What the Heck?" muttered Snuggles in disbelief. Clem's jaw dropped, then he smiled, "Great Kididdle-Hoppers, Granddaddy Clopper said it was all true and look, its blue!"

Above the full blue moon, they all watched the lights of Elysium & the big dipper shine brighter and brighter, until finally they lit up the entire night sky above Shasta. They could also see appear the bright tail of a large comet streaking across the night sky, just as it had been foretold so long ago.

"It's the 'Lights of Elysium' that great Granddaddy Clopper told me about. I never dreamed them to be so beautiful." Old Clem said in amazement.

"After 10,000 years, it's the return of the blue moon of Elysium that was foretold by the Presence." said Pigasus. Unisus told me all about it when I was growing up.

As they gazed into the sky, the distant silhouette of Unisus appeared in the "Lights of Elysium" and she flew towards the valley. "It's Unisus, she's back." said Snuggle Bunny, obviously still enchanted by her beauty.

They all watched, as Unisus flew towards the ranch and landed near the house. Snuggle Bunny didn't hesitate, he was off scampering across the grass, over the bridge hopping as fast as he could to get to Unisus.

Ruth gave them a good night kiss and turned out the lantern. But, before Becky & Mawdy could fall asleep, the lightning flashed, and the exploding thunder scared them very much. Unisus must have known something special, as she magically appeared at Becky's window. She took one look at the beautiful Unisus, her rainbow colored wings, long flowing golden mane, tail & magical golden horn and Becky smiled, as big a smile, as was ever possible. Then she opened her window and introduced herself to Unisus. "Hello, my name is Becky, and this is Mawdy."

"Hello Becky! Hello Mawdy! My name is Unisus." No sooner had Unisus introduced herself, when Snuggle Bunny came leaping through the window and landed on the bed next to Becky. "I'm Snuggle Bunny!" he said, as his back foot started thumping on the pillow. They all laughed and Unisus smiled at him and winked. "But of course, you are!" Snuggle was again twitterpatted and speechless but embarrassed about introducing himself again.

Unisus just smiled then turned to Becky and said, "The Presence has sent you a gift. He loves you Becky! He has heard your prayers." Then Unisus took her beautiful golden tail and waved it over Becky's doll. Little sparkles of gold dust sprinkled down over Mawdy. They danced and swirled all around her. Then Mawdy's blue button eyes came alive with the light of the Presence. "Always remember Becky, God loves you and so do I."

Unisus watched and listened to the little voice of Becky's rag doll start to sing their favorite song, "All you need is Faith, Hope, Love, Family and a Rainbows and Roses Lullaby." As Mawdy sang, Snuggle Bunny couldn't take his eyes off of the beautiful Unisus, still clearly in bunny love.

When Mawdy finished her lullaby, Becky reached out and gently cuddled her rag doll. Amazingly, Mawdy whispers, "God loves you Becky and so do I." Then the light in Mawdy's eyes faded. Becky looked up to see Unisus smile, just as she vanishes from the window.

Becky smiled, as she crawled under the covers and gives Mawdy a goodnight kiss. Then she looked up to see Snuggle Bunny hop out the window in search of the beautiful Unisus. Becky laughed and said "Mawdy, I think that silly bunny is twitterpatted!" Then they both drifted off to Lollyland.

Snuggle Bunny found Unisus approaching the old tree out in the pasture, where Clem Clopper and Pigasus were lying down for the evening. Snuggle Bunny hopped as fast as a jack rabbit to catch up to her. Just as they both reached the tree, Clem and Pigasus jumped up in the excitement of seeing Unisus. Then, it happened.

As was foretold so long ago, after 10,000 years, the true blue moon of Elysium returned to Shasta valley and the lights of Elysium filled the sky above the ancient volcano. In the pasture, Clem, Snuggle and Pigasus watched as a small point of intense blue light appeared in the old oak. It grew larger and larger. Golden sparkles began to swirl within the blue light that soon spread throughout the heart of the old oak.

Unisus, Clem Clopper, Snuggle and Pigasus stood wide eyed, amazed and humbled as the loving light of the Presence became brilliantly bright. Suddenly, from within the light of the Presence, Unicorn and Pegasus leapt majestically from within the light and landed gracefully side by side in front of Pigasus.

Pegasus spoke first. "Since the beginning we have been the guardians of the paradise Elysium. To hold true all that is right. All that is good. All that is love. The loving light of the Presence has touched your life Pigasus. Touched your heart. You are the 'Special One' chosen from the world to do battle against the evil Rathvar."

Pigasus stepped closer to Unicorn and Pegasus. He stood before them and the light of the Presence overwhelmed by the fear of his fate. "Why me?" He wondered. "What can I do to stop Rathvar. I'm scared."

Unicorn smiled at her frightened little pig and said, "You are special Pigasus. You are not just a pig; you have been touched by the light of the Presence and He loves you. We love you. You know this in your heart to be true. Pigasus, believe in the loving light of the Presence. The light always illuminates the darkness and true love will always win."

Pigasus seemed to understand. But, before he could speak, Pegasus looked deep into his heart and spoke, "I am honored to know you my son. I am proud the Presence chose you. You must believe Pigasus. You must also try. Try with all your heart. You must believe and you must try, for if you do the Presence will light your way when you face the evil Rathvar." Then Unicorn & Pegasus gave Pigasus what was almost like a "Tuggle" each reassuringly nuzzling him close with their unconditional love.

Then Unisus spoke, "It is love, Pigasus that will win the battle you must fight. Love for all that is, all that was and all that is to be again. Your future is our fate. Believe Pigasus. Find faith in the loving light of the Presence, in His love for all in the world and in His love for you Pigasus. The choice will be yours. You are the 'special one' chosen from the world to do battle against the evil Rathvar. We all love you Pigasus, your friends love you and most special of all the Presence loves you. Pigasus, believe in the loving light of the Presence."

Pigasus became overwhelmed with emotion. He stood tall and proud that Unicorn and Pegasus had so much faith in him. Clem and Snuggle Bunny were proud of him. "You can do it!" Snuggle blurted out. Pigasus smiled back at them knowing they all believed in him and that made him feel very special.

There was a moment of silence. Pigasus turned back to face Unicorn, Pegasus and the Presence. As he gazed deep into the light of the Presence, he heard a voice. "With the Faith to Believe in Love — Life becomes Magic".

As the light of the Presence vanished, Unicorn, Pegasus and Unisus vaulted into the night sky towards Mt. Shasta. Guided by the light of the full blue moon they headed for the shimmering blue light of the portal, which had reappeared on the mountain. Unicorn, Pegasus and Unisus flew back into Elysium.

Pigasus, Clem and Snuggle Bunny stood in the pasture, watching in silent fascination, as they heard the mighty roar of Rintrah from atop Mt. Shasta. "Rrrooaarrr!"

Then, the light of the full blue moon faded, giving way to a full lunar eclipse. The blackness of the darkness consumed the full blue moon and turned it to an ominous blood red moon. The cold wind began to blow, and a small dark cloud appeared above Shasta.

The darkness grew and they heard the distant thunder from the black lightning crashing through the night sky. It was Rathvar. As the remaining light vanished, Clem, Snuggles and Pigasus nestled close together and nervously fell fast asleep.

As the evil darkness grew, Pigasus began to dream. Not of Elysium, but a dark dream. Pigasus saw the Bennett's family farm now in ruins. George, Ruth, Johnny, Becky and Mawdy were all gone! Old Amostis was gone and even his bestest friends old Clem Clopper & Snuggle Bunny were gone. In the distance Unicorn & Pegasus are standing side by side, tears in their eyes and comforting one another.

Pigasus now had tears in his eyes, clearly troubled by the devastation. He wondered how the Presence could ever allow the blackness of the darkness that is the evil Rathvar destroy their home.

Then the light of the Presence appeared in his dream. Pigasus saw Unicorn and Pegasus smile and fly off to the lost paradise that still existed in the light of the Presence. It was then he realized the dark dream of Rathvar could still be undone. Pigasus woke up now understanding not to be scared of the dark, when you believe in the love of the light.

A small tear appeared in the sleepy eye of Pigasus and Snuggle awoke to see his friends tear. He quietly wiped the tear from the cheek of Pigasus, smiled, and gave him numerous warm 'Tuggles'.

As they lay there quietly sleeping, the blackness of the darkness was spreading. Once again black lightning flashed across the night sky and the sound of thunder rumbled through Shasta Valley. The blackness of the darkness was nearly complete, bringing the evil Rathvar ever nearer.

The next morning brought a dark and stormy day. A cold shiver awoke Clem Clopper that next morning and he knew this day was like no other. He felt the evil of Rathvar in the air. It was everywhere. Snuggle then opened his eyes as Clem rose and looked towards the mountain. Snuggle too realized something was wrong. It scared him a little and he snuggled close to Pigasus who was still asleep.

The sound of thunder filled the air. Pigasus awoke sensing the darkness of Rathvar and he slowly stood. They all looked up at the ancient volcano and saw the darkness that surrounded the now barren slopes and the raging dark thunderstorm consuming Shasta.

"It's a very stormy day." Snuggle said. "It's a very dark day." Clem said in a low ominous tone. Pigasus looked over at his two friends and then across the stormy sky. As he saw a very large bolt of black lightning crash directly into the West crater of Shasta he spoke, "It's a dark and stormy day."

Pigasus & Snuggle Bunny looked at each other and the hair on Snuggles back was standing on end. That made Pigasus smile and Snuggle quickly realized what he was smiling about and humbly smiled back. It made them both feel much more relaxed.

They decided to head for the house. As they got near the pond, Pigasus saw Amostis on his front porch with Dawg. He had never actually met Amostis, so they ran over to him. "Hi! I'm Pigasus!"

As they sat there Amostis said "Lordy, Lordy! A pig with wings!" just then his eyes turned brilliantly blue with the light of the Presence. "You are special! Believe Pigasus, Believe!" It was amazing. As the light in his eyes faded, Amostis just smiled. Then old Dawg howled and ran off towards the house, as Pigasus and Snuggle Bunny went on their way.

Back at the ranch Johnny and Becky were awake and looking out the window. Becky was holding Mawdy close and Dawg was now at Johnny's feet, his hand rested reassuringly on his head. They too realized it was a dark and stormy day.

A gust of bitter cold wind came through the window and they could hear the dark whispers of Rathvar. "Go to the pasture, Becky go visit Amostis." She told Johnny they must go to the pasture now and ran outside. Johnny hurried after her.

"Oh, I do hope Pigasus is well." Becky told Mawdy. "We have to go see Amostis."

It was then that they saw the black lightning flash from the large dark storm, strike the depths of the Mt. Shasta's crater. A gust of very strong wind rushed across the valley and blew Mawdy right out of Becky's hand and onto the ground.

"Oh Mawdy, are you all right." Becky hurried down picking Mawdy up and held her close.

As they approached the pond the wind blew very hard and again carried the voice of the evil Rathvar. "Believe! Believe in the darkness!"

They saw Amostis near the pond and began running over to meet him. When they reached him Amostis greeted them very strangely? "Well hello my little ones. Want some Hoghound candy for breakfast?" Amostis had given Johnny candy many times before. It's his favorite, but, never for breakfast and Amostis had always called Johnny and Becky by name.

Johnny notices that it seems a little darker than usual and Becky noticed that Amostis doesn't have that 'twinkle' in his eye. Instead there was a strange darkness. But still, Hoghound candy sounded pretty good and even though Johnny knew it was much too early to eat candy, he ate his anyway.

Becky finally had to admit she didn't like Hoghound candy. "Hoghound candy tastes yuckkkky." She said with a very sour look on her face.

The eyes of Amostis got very dark. "You'll like this candy. Believe! Becky, believe!" She was deceived to believe she would and so she ate hers too.

Johnny realized it wasn't Hoghound candy and as he looked up at Amostis he saw the blackness of the darkness in his eyes and realized that it wasn't Amostis at all. He spit the tainted candy out on the ground, but it was too late. He looked over at his sister just as she fell to the ground.

Johnny asked, "Who are you?" As Johnny fell to the ground he looked up and saw the image of Amostis transform into the blackness of the darkness. It was the evil Rathvar.

As they lay there, a strong cold wind blew the evil across Johnny and Becky. The blackness of the darkness rose into the sky and joined with the strange dark storm above the volcano Shasta. As it did, black lightning struck the East peak again and the sound of thunder rumbled through the valley below.

Johnny and Becky got up and started to walk back towards the house. Becky is holding Mawdy by her side. She is lifeless, dangling by one arm. Becky has a blank stare on her face and a strange darkness in her eyes.

Johnny followed by her side. He, too, had a strange darkness in his eyes. It was as though they were sleep walking in a strange trance. The Hoghound candy they had been given by the deceiving image of Amostis was POISION, tainted with the fever of darkness.

As they reached the front of the ranch, old Dawg let out a tremendously sad howl. "Arrooohhhhhhh!" George knew this howl of Dawg and he came running. There he stood looking at the dark lifeless eyes of his children and in that single moment realized how he longed for the light, which he had always taken for granted.

He picked up Becky and took Johnny by the arm. Becky had dropped Mawdy and as George headed inside, old Dawg gently picked up Mawdy in his mouth and followed them inside.

Ruth saw George rush by into the children's bedroom. She knew something was desperately wrong and followed them in. She dropped to her knees at the bedside of her little Becky, as George lay her gently on the bed. Ruth saw the darkness in her eyes, where there had always been the love of the light and she started to cry. "Oh George, George."

George had placed his only son, whom he loved so very much, on the bed next to Becky's and knelt close to his wife. "Oh George" Ruth said with tears in her eyes. They both realized the fever of darkness was consuming their children and there was nothing either of them could do.

George reached over and picked up Mawdy and laid her next to Becky. George then took Johnny's hand and Ruth brushed the hair from Becky's face and then held her hand. George looked at Ruth and put his arm lovingly around his wife saying, "Have faith Ruthie, have faith."

Ruth looked up at George and said, "Oh George, I love you so much!" She looked at him lovingly and then humbly lowered her head in prayer. George watched and wished there was something he could do but could only hold them close. A silent tear streamed down his face and his head fell in sadness. He wished he could believe.

Outside the ranch, throughout the valley Shasta it was the darkest of days. The cold wind blew hard, blowing over bushes and trees. The sky grew very dark and the storm above Shasta grew ever stronger, spreading across the sky.

Back in the pasture, Pigasus, Snuggle Bunny and old Clem watched the storm grow. Clem could never remember a day this dark and the storm was unlike any he had ever seen. "Great grand-daddy Clopper once told me about a storm like this, but I always thought he was just telling stories."

Snuggle nestled up to old Clem. It almost seemed as though the wind would blow him away. He looked up at Clem, over at Pigasus and then up at the mountain. The lightning crashed regularly across the mountains. He looked back over at Pigasus, "Is it him?" Snuggle asked cautiously.

Pigasus looked up at the dark clouds and he started to see an ominous black pulsating void in the darkest part of the storm. It was centered between the peaks of the volcano Shasta and as it grew, the light of day was turning darker. "It's him." Pigasus said in an almost calm knowing way. "It's Rathvar!"

By afternoon the dark storm began to engulf Shasta valley. Pigasus, Snuggle Bunny and Clem Clopper were out by the old oak. As the rain & wind darkened the sky, the loud crackle from a mas-sive bolt of black lightning flashed striking very near them.

Old Clem jumped back as the booming thunder shook the ground. Snuggle Bunny & Pigasus leapt into each other's arms in fear, then clumsily fell to the ground.

Silence followed. It was then, that the sudden increase in the amount of lightning brought their attention back to the sky. Towards Shasta, outlined in the darkness, was the beautiful Unisus. The lightning crashed through the sky and nearly struck her. She flew closer and closer. As she did, the wind blew even harder and the black lightning continued to arc through her path.

As Unisus was about to land she yelled down to them, "Beneath the sacred oak there is shelter." As Snuggle and Pigasus slowly got to their feet, Unisus lands next to them. They all came over to the tree. As they went beneath its sheltering limbs, the wind stopped. It was true, the storm raged throughout the lands, but not beneath the sacred oak.

"It's Rathvar! Pigasus, its time. You must confront him before he strikes again!" Unisus was clearly anxious and scared.

"You must believe Pigasus. The day of futures past is at hand." Unisus was very serious as she spoke directly to Pigasus.

"But, what can I do? I'm only one pig and I'm sca-sca-scared." Pigasus was truly upset. "I don't know what to do."

With love in her eyes she looked into Pigasus's big blue eyes and said "You've but to believe Pigasus. Never lose hope. Never lose faith. Believe in the love that is in your heart. It is there that your power lives. You've but to believe Pigasus. Believe in the love of the light." Unisus said reassuringly.

"Pigasus, find the faith to believe in yourself and in the loving light of the Presence. You must trust and know that "With the Faith to Believe in Love – Life becomes Magic!"

Pigasus looked up at Unisus, then sat down with his head hung low. He looked up at Unisus, over at Clem, then Snuggle. "I can't Unisus! It can't be me, I'm just a little pig. It just can't be me. I can't defeat Rathvar. I'm too scared!" Ears drooping and a tear in his eye, Pigasus lowers his head in shame.

They all looked at Pigasus, not knowing what to say or do. Then all of a sudden, another brilliant bolt of Black Lightning lit up the entire sky, then another and another. The thunder was deafening and clearly, they were all centered between the towering peak and rugged crater of the Mt. Shasta.

A new darkness began to rise. It was the full moon rising amidst the storm. As the sun was setting in the West, the moon was rising in the East. As it ascended to its apex atop the volcano Shasta it began to eclipse. It quickly became very dark, then turned an ominous blood red, where the blue moon of Elysium had been only the night before. Unlike any other, this eclipse created a "Dark Moon", like a black hole in the sky. It became the black moon of darkness.

Then all of a sudden "Rrrooaarrrrrr!" It came from Shasta, from between the peaks, Unisus heard the mighty roar of Rintrah. The roar thundered through the valley Shasta and then "Rrrooaarrrrrr!" was heard again. The storm raged on and black lightning continued crashing through the peaks.

It was the mighty Rintrah! As they all turned their attention to the mountain, they saw Rintrah soaring beneath the East peak of Shasta, towards the center of the dark storm above the crater. More Black Lightning crackled through the sky, targeting Rintrah as he dove, swerved and again they hear, "Rrrooaarrrr!"

An eerie dark, orange glow grew from the depths of the darkness in the cave at the base of the Crater and both Snuggle Bunny and Pigasus knew it was the Evil Rathvar. The storm raged and Rintrah roared again as he flew fearlessly towards the blackness of the darkness! Rathvar emerged from the cave, clearly to confront the mighty Rintrah. Then it happened, a huge bolt of Black Lightning struck Rintrah! It stopped him in mid-air, then Rintrah hovered for a moment, then struck back.

Rintrah reared back, his mighty wings arched in front of him, his piercing blue eyes glowing brightly and with a deafening roar, mighty bolts of Blue Lightning seemed to emanate from the heavens above, thru his wingtips and rocketed into the blackness of the darkness that was Rathvar. But, Rathvar had grown too strong for Rintrah to defeat him.

As the aerial battle raged on, Unisus realized that indeed Pigasus would be unable to save them and Rintrah needed her help. Through the dark storm and flashes of black lightning, they could all see the silhouette of the mighty Rintrah battling Rathvar, who had grown in strength and now seemed to engulf the entire mountain.

Unisus and Pigasus could not believe their eyes when they saw Rintrah vanish in the void of darkness. They waited for him to fly back out. They waited a moment and then there was an incredible surge in the black storm followed by multiple bursts of lightning.

Every few strikes were brilliant blue flashes, which they were sure must have been from the mighty Rintrah. The blue flashes faded and the realm of Rathvar grew. There was only black lightning now and as the thunder rolled through the valley Shasta, they could hear the evil voice of Rathvar howling thru the wind, "Believe in the darkness, Pigasus, believe in the darkness."

Unisus now too believed Pigasus couldn't defeat Rathvar, so she was going to confront him. "Believe in the light Pigasus. Believe in the loving light of the Presence. He believes in you. I believe in you. I love you Pigasus!"

With that Unisus bolted into the sky toward the mountain to save her lifelong friend and trusted companion. "Rintrah! Rintrah!" she called as the black lightning of Rathvar struck all around her.

As Unisus raced towards the Blackness of the Darkness, Pigasus cried out, "Unisus, No!! Don't leave me." But, Unisus was determined to help Rintrah and save Pigasus from his fate. Pigasus watched helplessly as Unisus flew towards the Evil Rathvar.

From the valley below, Snuggle Bunny came bravely from behind Clem. He was clearly in a rage. "You don't hurt her you mean old Rathvar or I'll --- I'll." He started to move out from under the tree, "I'll have to hurt you!" With that he started doing bunny kicks. "Tha-Pah, Tha-Pah."

Pigasus could hear Snuggles voice fade as the cold voice of Rathvar filled the air. "Believe in the darkness, the darkness."

As Unisus approached the blackness that was consuming Shasta, Rathvar tried to strike her with bolts of Black Lightning, but she galloped and flew through the raging storm, leaving a swirling trail of magical gold dust behind her, finally landing on the cliff above the cave. But, Unisus was immediately struck by a powerful bolt of Black Lightning that engulfed her in Darkness, trapping her on the cliff above the cave in Rathvar's grasp.

The dark voice of Rathvar spoke "Believe! Unisus, believe in the darkness!"

"Never!" she cried. "I will never believe in the darkness and neither will Pigasus. He is the special one, chosen because his heart is true. His faith is strong! He is a true believer, whose faith in the loving light of the Presence is stronger than you Rathvar."

Unisus then heard the sinister laughter of Rathvar, "Ha, Ha, Ha! He will believe! Believe in the blackness of the darkness!" As the voice of Rathvar faded, the storm above Shasta grew ever darker and the black lightning crashed all around the valley and continually striking near Unisus.

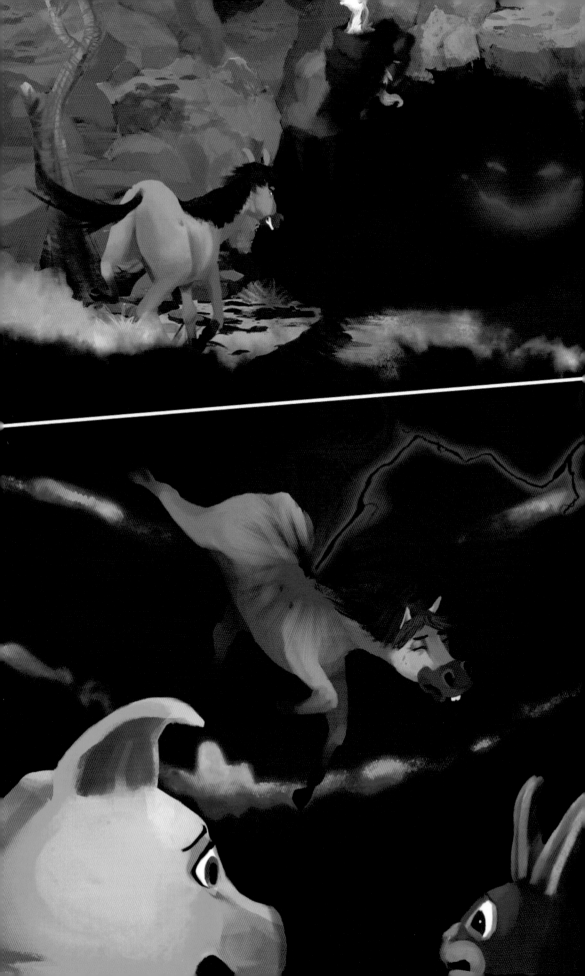

Pigasus, Snuggle Bunny and Clem saw the whole thing. Snuggle Bunny knew he had to save Unisus and started to hop towards the mountain. Pigasus started to follow and then Clem. Like never before they raced towards the mountain and up the side. Snuggle and Pigasus became exhausted and Clem caught up to them about halfway up the mountain.

Clem put Pigasus and Snuggle Bunny on his back and carried them up the remainder of the volcano Shasta until they reached the cave at the base of the cliff below Unisus and the evil Rathvar. Clem stopped and let Pigasus and Snuggle off and Snuggle was ready to go on and began to fearlessly start hopping forward. As he did, a large bolt of black lightning crashed at Snuggles feet stopping him in his tracks.

Then, as Pigasus hears the cry of Unisus, he has an epiphany and now realizes what he must do, save Unisus. But old Clem Clopper had already started gallantly galloping up the cliff edge. Pigasus yelled up to Clem, "Be careful Clem."

"Have faith Pigasus. Believe!" Clem smiled and turned to face the evil Rathvar. As he leaped to save Unisus, lightning crashed at his feet and then a massive devastating bolt of Black Lightning struck old Clem Clopper and sent him flying head over heels high into the blackness of the darkness.

As Clem stood back up, Pigasus & Snuggle Bunny started towards Clem to help, but, watched helplessly, as they saw him get struck by another devastating bolt of Black Lightning and the lifeless body of old Clem Clopper vanished into the depths of the darkness.

Pigasus stopped dead in his tracks, heartbroken at the death of Old Clem. Pigasus and Snuggle Bunny couldn't believe their eyes. Clem Copper was truly gone, lost forever in the depths of the darkness.

Snuggle became overwhelmed with emotion and stormed up the side of the cliff as Pigasus pleaded for him not to go. Snuggle turned to Pigasus, "I have to save Unisus." He turned and continued. "Come out and fight Rathvar." Snuggle said as he kicked into the air several times. "Tha-Pah! Tha-Pah!"

The storm raged on and Lightning struck near Snuggle Bunny. It sent him head over heels down the side of the rocky cliff. Snuggle stopped at the feet of Pigasus and looked up at him. Pigasus looked down at Snuggle with a tear in his eye. "Oh, Snuggle. It's all my fault. If only I were brave. Now Clem's gone!" He hung his head almost ashamed that he could be responsible for the perilous fate which had hurt all of his friends.

Snuggle looked up at his friend and just before he passed out from the bump on his head he said, "I believe in you Pigasus, I believe."

As Pigasus fights back the tears, he realizes the love of his friends, their selfless sacrifice to protect him by confronting the evil Rathvar have left no doubt in his heart. Love is faith and that no matter what happens, he must have the faith to believe in love. Pigasus now knows he is ready to embrace his fate.

Pigasus looked deep into Snuggle Bunny's eyes and as they closed, he saw a faint glimmer of the light of Elysium. He raised his head and looked up towards the crater's edge and at the dark storm that raged above the mountain. He saw Unisus trapped in the Blackness of the Darkness "Not to my friends, I'll never believe in you, never!"

As it was foretold, Pigasus takes a leap of faith, jumping right over the top of Snuggle Bunny. Leaping into the sky he yells "I'm coming Unisus!" Pigasus could only think of saving Unisus. Then, the brilliant blue light of the Presence began to shine in his eyes. It was clear the fate of Elysium now rested in the heart of a true believer.

Pigasus becomes immediately strong, confident and courageous as he flew boldly towards the cliff below the craters edge and the evil Rathvar. As he did, black lightning struck all around him and the cold wind howled.

He flew through the raging storm towards the Blackness of the Darkness, where Pigasus knew he would confront the evil Rathvar. The winds howled and bolts of Black Lightning were striking all around him. But Pigasus was relentless as he charged towards Rathvar. The Battle for Evermore had begun.

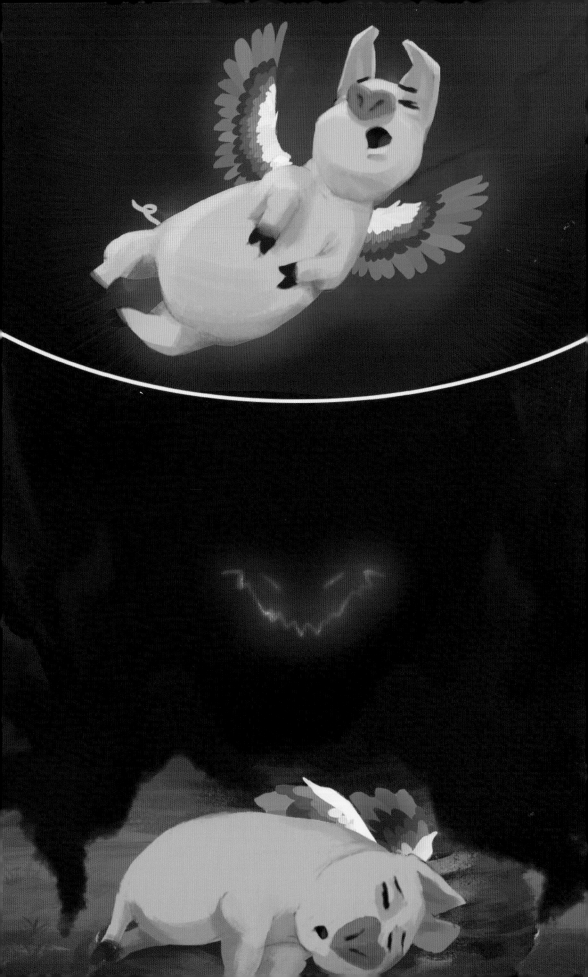

The black lightning of Rathvar struck Pigasus and sent him crashing into the ground in front of the cave. Clearly hurting, he laid there next to Snuggle Bunny. Looking down at his nearly defeated friend, tears appeared in Snuggles eyes, as he thought all was surely lost. The cold wind again carried the voice of Rathvar. "Believe Pigasus, Believe in the darkness."

Pigasus slowly opened his eyes and looked over at Snuggle and thought of his lost friend Clem Clopper whom he had just watch die. He thought of the beautiful Unisus trapped in the blackness of the darkness. Pigasus thought he was somehow responsible and for the first time in his life Pigasus felt the overwhelming weight of hopelessness.

The roar of the wind raged through Pigasus. "Believe Pigasus! Take me through the portal to Elysium. Save Unisus! Believe
in the darkness." Rathvar was offering Pigasus a chance to
save Unisus. All he had to do was guide him through the lost
portal to Elysium. The voice of Rathvar was like a glimmer of
hope. Pigasus felt he had to listen.

But, Pigasus was determined to save Unisus who was clearly now struggling to
survive. Pigasus again leaped into the
air flying towards Unisus. But just
before he reached the cliff's edge, he
was struck down by a massive bolt
of Black Lightning and crashed
into the entrance of the cave
below, seemingly lifeless. But as
his head cleared, Pigasus stood
up looking for Unisus. But all
he saw was the blackness of
the darkness, as he stood
unafraid in front of the
raging Rathvar.

Suddenly, Pigasus saw a strange vision, it was Elysium, but burning and in ruins. Rathvar's voice whispered on the wind. "Pigasus, you can save
Elysium. Just say you believe in
me. You can save Unisus just
walk into the darkness. Clem
Clopper is there. You can save him,
come Pigasus, join me."

Pigasus knew it was a trick and said
"No, I will never go with you!" As he spoke, the
vision became the light of the Presence, when
Pigasus got his wings, his name and his heart. He
remembered what the Presence said to him. "With
the Faith to Believe in Love - Life becomes Magic!"

Pigasus defiantly looked into the blackness of the darkness that was Rathvar and said, "No! You don't scare me anymore and you can't deceive me into believing in your darkness. I believe in the Presence and the light. He loves me and I believe! He told me good always defeats evil, if you have faith!"

As Pigasus confronted Rathvar, the light of the Presence began to appear behind him in the opening of the cave and grew stronger and brighter with every word Pigasus spoke. "I have Faith Rathvar and you are Evil!"

With those words Rathvar's rage became out of control and black lightning began striking everywhere. Pigasus knew Unisus was near death and now was his time. This is his destiny. With a determined look, Pigasus repeated the words of the Presence, "With the Faith to Believe in Love - Life becomes Magic!"

Then Pigasus reared back on his hind legs and arched his wingtips forward, just as he had seen the mighty Rintrah do. As his wingtips touched, Pigasus lunged forward and a bolt of blue lightning arched through the blackness of the darkness.

As it did, Pigasus fell awkwardly backwards. Behind him, the intense light of the Presence became blinding. As he rolled over onto his belly, a brilliant bolt of blue lightning arched through the cave into the very essence of the evil Rathvar. It radiated into a thousand smaller lightning bolts arching through the darkness. As the brilliant blast faded, so too had the evil Rathvar.

Pigasus stood up in awe, thinking he had destroyed Rathvar, but he quickly remembered Unisus and rushed out to see her slowly standing up atop the cliff.

"Pigasus! Pigasus, where are you?" It was coming from the cliff above the cave. He looked up towards the crater's edge and a big smile came across his face, "Unisus! Oh, Unisus! You're all right!" It was true, it was Unisus who leaped from cliff above the once dark cave below the crater's edge. Pigasus lovingly watched Unisus, as she gracefully landed next to him. She smiled as she looked over and saw Snuggle Bunny up and hopping happily towards them.

"I'll save you Unisus!" Snuggles shouted. But realizing Unisus had already been saved, he became very embarrassed.

Unisus simply smiled, "I'm very proud of you Pigasus. Proud of both of you! You were both very, very brave." Snuggle stood proud, with one paw beginning to thump on the ground with a big bunny smile looking up into the big beautiful eyes of Unisus. Yep, Snuggles was Twitterpatted again.

"Pigasus, you did it! You've saved us all!" said Unisus.

"I did?" he humbly replied. "Yes, Pigasus! You had the Faith to believe in Love."

Then Unisus & Snuggles realized something was still wrong as they saw Pigasus starring sadly up at the crater's edge, desperately hoping to see old Clem Clopper. "Clem? Clem? Are you up there too Clem?" Pigasus said as a tear rolled down his cheek.

Unisus looked sadly at Pigasus with tears welling up in her eyes, as she knew Clem wasn't coming back. Snuggles too realized Pigasus had not forgotten about the courageous Clem Clopper, who had so bravely given his life to try and save Unisus. Snuggle Bunny hopped over next to Pigasus and slid his big old ears under his cheeks to give him a tuggle.

"Oh Snuggles, why couldn't I have been brave like Clem" Pigasus said sadly. "Maybe old Clem would still be alive."

Snuggles looked up at Pigasus, both remembering how they weren't brave enough to go with old Clem to save Unisus and wondered if they had been brave, would Clem Clopper be alive. "Isn't Clem ever coming back?" Snuggles innocently asked.

Pigasus and Snuggle Bunny both had big old tears well up in their eyes, one rolling down the chubby cheek of Pigasus onto Snuggles ear. Unisus who knew old Clem Clopper was gone forever, also had tears well up in her eyes. Unisus nuzzled her nose into Snuggle Bunny's ears and across Pigasus's cheeks and they all closed their eyes, quietly tuggling each other thinking about how much they all loved old Clem Clopper.

Unisus then raised her head and looked deep into Pigasus's big teary blue eyes, "Pigasus, there is nothing we can do for Clem. He is gone." Unisus said in a soft caring voice.

Pigasus said with a tear in his eye. "But, it's not fair Unisus. He should be here with us. Clem never ever hurt anyone. He was only trying to protect us and save you!"

Unisus, still looking deep into Pigasus's eyes lovingly replied, "Don't be sad, Pigasus. Clem is with the Presence, who has always loved him very much. You should be very proud of Clem. He has always had the faith to believe in the loving light of the Presence and old Clem Clopper always loved you."

"There is magic in the air tonight Pigasus" Unisus said in mysterious way. "Thanks to you. You're very special Pigasus. You are a true believer." Pigasus wasn't sure what to say, but it was both comforting and very humbling as he smiled back. With those words, Unisus vaulted into the air and began to fly towards the pasture in the valley below.

All of a sudden, "Rrrrooooaaaarrrrr" They heard the mighty roar of Rintrah. "Rrrrrooooaaaarrr".

Pigasus looked at Snuggles, who looked back at him and started to smile as Pigasus proudly stood tall and said in a very confident voice, "Hop on Snuggles, we're going for a little ride." But, Snuggle looked a little skeptical until he saw a glimmer of blue light sparkle in the eyes of Pigasus.

It was then he knew Pigasus was both capable and proud of his big beautiful "Pig Wings" and his unique gift of flight. Snuggle Bunny grinned from Big Ear to Big Ear and hopped up on Pigasus, positioning himself between his rainbow colored wings.

Then remembering Clem's words, Snuggles laughed "Pigs really do fly!" Then yells, "Getty-up Pigasus, Getty-up. Weeee-Haaah!"

Pigasus leaped into the air and proudly flew towards the Shasta valley. Behind them was the towering Mt. Shasta and above the brilliantly shining full blue moon had returned. They landed gracefully near the sacred oak tree where Unisus now stood.

She was looking across the pasture at the ranch where the Bennett family was still gathered in Becky & Johnny's bedroom, who were still deathly ill from eating the "Evil Hoghound" candy that poisoned them.

"Look Pigasus, it's the "Lights of Elysium." Unisus said excitedly looking high in the night sky above Shasta.

As she does, we see the "Lights of Elysium", shining brightly in the twilight sky just above the full blue moon and in front of the "Big Dipper". Unisus smiled, "There will be a new true believer tonight."

Pigasus knew somehow that the new true believer would be George. He looked over at the ranch and smiled, "It is magic to believe, isn't it Unisus?"

Unisus just smiled and gazed across the pasture to the house, where she could see the loving light of the Presence began to shine in the children's bedroom. George and Ruth were at Becky & Johnny's bedside, both still deathly ill from eating the evil Hoghound candy that poisoned them.

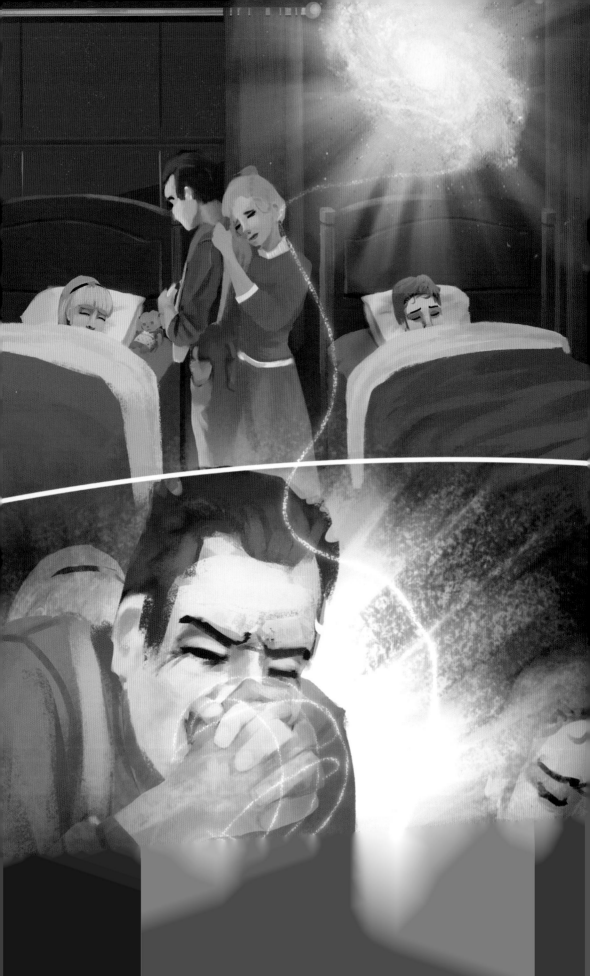

There in the bedroom, George is on his knees next to Ruth at the foot of Becky's bed, where she and Johnny were near death. Behind him in the upper corner of the room, the light of the Presence appeared as George began to pray for the first time since he was a boy.

"Dear God, I've never been a praying man, but Lord, please save my son and my little girl. Dear God, Please!" A tear rolled down George's cheek, as he lowered his head further in faith.

As he prayed, the loving light of the Presence grew, and a flash of blue lightning struck George's heart. Johnny awoke and smiled as Dawg licked his face. Becky awoke and hugged Mawdy and then her mother. George's eyes were still closed in silent prayer. He raised his head and opened his eyes gazing up towards the light of the Presence.

His loving light reflected in his eyes, as the Presence had touched the hardened heart of George Bennett. He looked back toward his wife and saw the smiling faces of Johnny, Becky and even Mawdy as they all rushed over to hug him. A tearful glimmer of His loving light was shining in the eyes of the Bennett family. The Presence answered George's prayer and saved Johnny & Becky.

Outside the window, Becky sees the full blue moon shining bright above Shasta. The storm is gone and the 'Lights of Elysium' are shining brightly above a magical rainbow. "Look Mawdy! It's like a Rainbow, God's promise that everything will all be right."

As Becky looks down at Mawdy we see a "Twinkle" in Mawdy's eyes like when she came alive to sing to her. Becky knows it's the loving light of the Presence because Becky has always had the faith to believe.

Then suddenly, in the distance, they heard Amostis yelling from out towards the pasture, "Lordy, Lordy, come and see the miracle". Then Dawg howled, "A-Roooh-Rooh-Rooohhhh!"

The Bennett family hurried out the door and joined Amostis in running to the base of the old oak as the Presence began to appear.

The dark storm and the rage of Rathvar was gone. The "Lights of Elysium" were shining brightly in the night sky just above the full blue moon centered above the ancient twin volcano. There, just in front of the "Big Dipper", a most wondrous sight occurred. A beautifully rare 'midnight rainbow' arched brilliantly across the sky.

"Daddy, Mawdy look! Wow!" Becky yelled pointing towards Shasta. "Look Mawdy, Look! Flying horses!"

George, Ruth and Johnny see the Presence appearing for the FIRST Time. They start walking towards the light and as they get close, they are astounded to see Unisus and Pigasus, with Snuggle Bunny in front of the Oak.

As if that weren't spectacular enough, they are amazed to actually see Unisus for the first time and that "their pet pig" actually does have rainbow colored WINGS!

Becky smiles and tells Mawdy sarcastically "See Mawdy, Pigasus does have wings" and then she makes Mawdy say to Johnny sarcastically "Told you so!" which made everyone laugh.

Becky see's in the distance, above the ancient Shasta the outline of Unicorn & Pegasus flying towards them, the full Blue Moon & the lights of Elysium shining brightly behind them. They gracefully land in front of the Oak beside Unisus & Pigasus, where the light of the Presence is now brilliant, as are the stars, the full blue moon and the lights of Elysium.

Unicorn and Pegasus magically stood in the light of the Presence and proudly in front of Pigasus. But, before they could say anything, Unicorn and Pegasus could see sadness had quickly overtaken this joyous moment.

Pigasus sadly turns toward the heart of the ancient oak and looks directly into the Light of the Presence with his sad teary "blue" eyes and says, "Clem's Gone!" Tears welling up in his eyes, "If only I could have had the faith to believe sooner, I could have saved him!"

There was a brief moment of silence, as Pigasus hung his head in shame, a big teardrop fell to the ground. Everyone realizes old Clem Clopper is gone.

Pigasus turned away from the light and walked away from his family. They all realized Pigasus wanted to have Clem Clopper back. Everyone got very sad. Ruth and Becky had tears in their eyes and so did Unisus.

Pigasus kept walking with his head hung low and then stopped near the piece of dug up pasture where he had first met Clem. With a big old tear in his eyes Pigasus says "I love you Clem Clopper."

Pigasus then looked up to see Amostis, who also had walked over towards the spectacular site of the Presence and was standing before him with his eyes brilliantly alive with the loving light of the Presence. Pigasus couldn't say a word to Amostis. The sadness of losing Clem overwhelmed him. Amostis looked deep into the heart of Pigasus and said, "With the Faith to Believe in Love – Life becomes Magic!"

"I have faith Amostis, I do believe. But I don't understand why old Clem Clopper had to die." He said as a big old tear fell where Clem had once stood. Just as the tear vanished into the grass, Pigasus raised his head, turned and looked into the light of the Presence. "I will" he said softly. "I will continue to believe. I will keep the faith. I do have the faith to believe in love! Old Clem was – he was – –"

All of a sudden, "Heeeeeee – – – !" It was the distinctive voice of old Clem Clopper! Pigasus raises his head, wide eyed and still staring into the eyes of Amostis. "Heee-Heee-Heee."

He heard Clem again and Pigasus smiles the biggest smile ever and turns to see old Clem leap right out from the heart of the Light of the Presence. Then standing proudly between Unicorn and Pegasus Clem proclaims, "Gall Darn! I've seen it! Elysium! I was there! It's AMAZING! Wee-Hah!!!

Pigasus was so excited to see Clem he rushed towards him, but clumsily trips, rolls and does one last pigstop right at old Clem Clopper's feet. As everyone begins to laugh, Pigasus jumps up and proclaims "Your Alive! Clem Your Alive!"

Old Clem leaned down and "Tuggles" Pigasus. Clem laughed and says, "Well of course I am!" Clem never realizes he "died", went to Elysium and the Presence brought him back to life. Pigasus smiled and says "I Love you Clem Clopper"

Clem smiles back and gives Pigasus a very special tuggle saying, "I love you too, Pigasus!"

Then the brilliant blue lightning of the Presence flashed and thundered rumbled across the valley causing both Clem and Pigasus to turn back towards the Presence.

As everyone stood facing the light, there is a moment of Silence and then the Presence speaks, "Pigasus, always remember, With the Faith to Believe in Love - Life becomes Magic"

Pigasus smiled maybe the biggest smile ever as he then knew, that they would all live happily ever after, because.

"With the Faith to Believe in Love Life becomes Magic!"

PIGASUS

THE LOST PARADISE ELYSIUM
BATTLE FOR EVERMORE

WITH THE FAITH TO BELIEVE IN LOVE
LIFE BECOMES MAGIC